SMOKE ON THE MOUNTAIN HOMECOMING

Written
by
CONNIE RAY

Conceived
by
ALAN BAILEY

Musical Arrangements
by
MIKE CRAVER

SAMUEL FRENCH, INC.

45 West 25th Street
NEW YORK 10010
LONDON

7623 Sunset Boulevard
HOLLYWOOD 90046
TORONTO

CHARACTERS

MERVIN OGLETHORPE – *Pastor Of Mount Pleasant Baptist Church, mid-30s*

The Sanders Family

BURL – *Father, 50*

VERA – *Mother, 50*

STANLEY – *Uncle, 50*

DENNIS – *Twin Brother, early 20s*

DENISE – *Twin Sister, early 20s*

JUNE – *Sister (and Mervin's wife), mid 20s*

SETTING

The play takes place in the sanctuary of the Mount Pleasant Baptist Church in Mount Pleasant, North Carolina, located just west of Hickory near the Blue Ridge Mountains. It is Saturday night, October 6, 1945, two months after VJ Day. The war is over, our boys are home, the Depression is a bad memory, and the baby boom has begun.

Mount Pleasant's principal industries are farming and pickle production. The Mount Pleasant Pickle Plant makes everyone and everything smell of vinegar and dill.

The Sanders Family first performed at Mount Pleasant Baptist on June 15, 1938 after a five-year hiatus from the Gospel Circuit. They returned to Mount Pleasant each year until the beginning of the war in 1941. This is their first performance in four years.

SONG LIST

ACT I

LEANING ON THE EVERLASTING ARMS....................Traditional
GLORYLAND BOOGIE..by Abner Buford
EVERYTHING YOU'LL NEED......................by Squire E. Parsons, Jr.
I'LL NEVER DIE..by Ila C. Knight
THE ROYAL TELEPHONE..Traditional
A LITTLE AT A TIME......................by Edd F. Easter, James Easter, and
                                                            Russell Lee Easter
CHILDREN TALK TO ANGELS..............................by Cleo B. Kirby
STANDING ON THE PROMISES..Traditional
RIVER MEDLEY
    SHALL WE GATHER AT THE RIVER........................Traditional
    I'M GOING TO CANAAN....................................by Alan Bailey
    YOU CAN SWIM..by Mike Craver
    FAR SIDE BANKS OF JORDAN............................by Terry Smith
I AM READY TO GO..by Early Upchurch

ACT II

COME AROUND...by Mike Craver
I'LL LIVE AGAIN..by Ila C. Knight
ROUND-UP IN THE SKY....................by Alan Bailey and Mike Craver
I LOVE TO TELL THE STORY..Traditional
PROPHET MEDLEY
    DANIEL IN THE LION'S DEN..............................by Alan Bailey
    EZEKIEL SAW THE WHEEL..Traditional
    WE ARE CLIMBING JACOB'S LADDER..................Traditional
    JOSHUA FIT THE BATTLE OF JERICHO..................Traditional
JESUS SAVIOR, PILOT ME...Traditional
JUST OVER IN THE GLORYLAND................................Traditional
UNCLOUDED DAY..Traditional
DO LORD..Traditional

PLAYWRIGHTS' NOTE

Smoke on the Mountain Homecoming, a comedy with music, takes place in 1945 at Mount Pleasant Baptist Church in Mount Pleasant, North Carolina. The play presents a Gospel Sing, using a cast of seven with the audience being the congregation.

Smoke on the Mountain Homecoming is the third in a series of plays. In the first, *Smoke on the Mountain,* Pastor Mervin Oglethorpe, a young and enthusiastic minister, enlists the Sanders Family Singers in his efforts to bring his tiny congregation into the "modern world." The second play, *Sanders Family Christmas,* takes place on Christmas Eve, 1941, just before young Dennis Sanders ships off to join World War II. In both plays, the family members "witness," or tell personal stories that relate to their trials of faith, between Gospel songs.

Production values should reflect the simplicity of the 1940s rural South. The setting should evoke a small Baptist church whose minister is paid so little that he has to take a part-time job at the local pickle plant. The costumes should likewise be appealing but plain.

Smoke on the Mountain Homecoming uses twenty-four standard gospel songs (all of which have been licensed for all future performances of the play). The actors who play the Sanders Family must be able to sing and play these songs — they are the only musicians in the production. Piano, guitar, and string bass are used in most songs — banjo, fiddle, autoharp, ukulele, and harmonica are instruments that could be added depending on the actors' skills. The actress playing June plays hand-held percussion instruments.

Because *Smoke on the Mountain Homecoming* is presentational — the event of the play is the Gospel Sing itself — it is essential that the play be directed as an ensemble piece. The main character of the play is the Sanders Family. Much of the story of the play and the establishment of relationships within the family is told through behavior rather than words. The acting style is naturalistic. These characters are not Southern caricatures or religious buffoons, but real people.

ACT I

(Lights are up on the sanctuary of Mount Pleasant Baptist, a small, rural, poor Southern Baptist church. It is 7:00 pm on Saturday, October 6, 1945. Onstage, there is a small empty choir loft, a piano, a small offering table, pews, a couple of chairs, and a pulpit. A black castiron stove sits in the corner. A plaque on the wall proclaims last Sunday's attendance and offering. One naked light bulb hangs center stage. There are two doors upstage, one leading to the pastor's study, one to the outside. Steps downstage allow the cast to enter from the house. The Sanders' instruments are scattered about the stage.

From the upstage door, STANLEY SANDERS ambles in, glances at the congregation, picks up a guitar, and begins to tune it. A few moments later, BURL and DENNIS SANDERS ENTER from the upstage door. DENNIS wears a suit and carries a Bible. BURL nods to the congregation and begins tuning a banjo. DENNIS walks to the pulpit, places his Bible, nods to the congregation, and moves down to tune a fiddle. After a moment, VERA SANDERS enters through the same door; the tuning abruptly stops. VERA huddles with BURL and DENNIS. STANLEY resumes soft strumming. VERA turns to glare at him. He stops. BURL motions to STANLEY to join the huddle. They form a circle and whisper to one another. The upstage door opens and DENISE SANDERS CULPEPPER sticks her head in. All attention goes to DENISE. She shakes her head "no". The Sanders motion her into the huddle. A decision is made.

VERA goes to sit behind the piano, DENISE sits close to the upstage window, and DENNIS goes to stand behind the pulpit. He smiles at the congregation.)

DENNIS. Well, I reckon Reverend Oglethorpe has set his watch to Texas time already. He was right behind us when we left the parsonage —

BURL. Right behind us one minute, then I look in the mirror and he was gone.

DENNIS. You all know Reverend Oglethorpe got the call to preach down in West Texas —

VERA. And taking June with him!

BURL. And taking our daughter June — *(Pointedly, to VERA.)* — his wife — with him.

VERA. Well.

DENNIS. But it's a puzzle where they got off to. We've come up from Siler City for a few days, helping Mervin and June pack up —

(BURL and VERA can't help jumping in trying to help DENNIS, even though it's clear from DENNIS's quiet composure that he doesn't need any help. DENNIS good-naturedly tolerates the interruptions.)

BURL. And bringing Dennis's things so he can settle in.

VERA. The Reverend Dennis Sanders.

BURL. We are so proud Dennis has been called to be the new minister here at Mount Pleasant Baptist.

VERA. The Divine Call.

BURL. Former chaplain of the United States Marine Corps.

VERA. And he's single!

DENNIS. There they are.

DENISE. *(To DENNIS.)* No, that's the twins playing in the yard. *(Knocking on the window.)* Weldon, Eldon, y'all be quiet for Mama, please. Thank you. *(To congregation, beaming.)* My little boys. They're three next month.

VERA. They are precious.

BURL. A twin having twins. Don't that beat all?

VERA. Twins run on my side of the family.

DENISE. We're letting them run off a little steam before they come and perform for you tonight. *(Shouting at door.)* Donnie, honey, don't let them play with the people's cars.

BURL. I gotta say you good folks at Mount Pleasant have been mighty generous to Reverend Oglethorpe. I know he didn't come here with much more than that plastic comb he's so fond of, but we have packed trunk after trunk, box upon box.

VERA. He won't throw away so much as a can lid.

BURL. And every time he picks something up, he needs to tell a little story —

VERA. — about who gave it to him and how much it means to him.

BURL. Their old car is so loaded down, the tires are spraddling out and he's got a trailer hitched to the back just brimming.

DENISE. He won't drive over twenty miles an hour 'cause of June. It's gonna take 'em two months to get to Texas.

VERA. If they haven't run off in a ditch already!

BURL. Now, Mother.

VERA. Well, he's got no business gallivanting across the country with June.

(The SANDERS start speaking over one another.)

DENISE. He's not the best driver, Daddy —
DENNIS. They just stopped to stretch their legs —
VERA. It's only three miles —
STANLEY. *(Cutting in.)* He went to see his Mama.

(All focus goes to STANLEY for a beat. Then –)

VERA. *(Quietly)* Oh, good Lord, yes.

(Long beat.)

BURL. *(To family.)* You know how old Mervin is about his Mama. He may never get here.

(The SANDERS move to huddle again when a noise from the back pulls DENNIS's attention.)

PASTOR OGLETHORPE. I'm sorry!
DENNIS. There he is!

(From the back of the house, PASTOR OGLETHORPE ENTERS at full speed, charging towards the stage. He carries a small pink overnight bag.)

PASTOR OGLETHORPE. I'm sorry. I'm so sorry. Oh, and you all sitting here waiting. Psalms 38:18, "For I will declare mine iniquity. I will be sorry for my sin."
VERA. Where's June?
PASTOR OGLETHORPE. June! Oh, my Mrs. Oglethorpe! She said to run ahead. Here she is!

(JUNE SANDERS OGLETHORPE ENTERS from the back of the house, briskly waddling toward the stage. She is enormously pregnant.)

JUNE. We're sorry. *(PASTOR OGLETHORPE rushes to JUNE and tries to help her along.)* I'm fine.
VERA. *(Scolding PASTOR OGLETHORPE.)* Matthew 25:5, "The bridegroom was a long time coming."
PASTOR OGLETHORPE. Matthew 27:23, "And they were exceedingly sorry." *(To JUNE.)* Now, take little steps. Don't rush yourself.
JUNE. I'm fine. *(She lumbers down the aisle with PASTOR OGLETHORPE.)* Uncle Stanley!
STANLEY. Hello, sweetheart. Look at you.

(JUNE hugs STANLEY as though she hasn't seen him for years. The SANDERS surround them; PASTOR OGLETHORPE stands to the side. As the family shuttles JUNE to a pew and settles her in, PASTOR OGLETHORPE approaches STANLEY. They regard one another for a beat and shake hands. DENISE chooses this moment to look out the back door for her children.)

VERA. *(Continuing to scold PASTOR OGLETHORPE.)* Luke 1:21, "And the people waited for Zacharias and marveled that he tarried so long."
PASTOR OGLETHORPE. John 16:20, "I am sorrowful, but my sorrow has turned to joy."

VERA. Numbers 22:37, "Did I not earnestly call you? Why did you not come to me?"

PASTOR OGLETHORPE. "Yea, sorrowful, sorrowful, but always rejoicing— "

PASTOR OGLETHORPE & VERA. - 2 Corinthians 6:10—

PASTOR OGLETHORPE. — Amen. Thank you, Mrs. Sanders. *(VERA lowers herself onto the piano bench as PASTOR OGLETHROPE lands behind the pulpit. Running a quick comb through his hair.)* Praise the Lord! This is what I call a Homecoming! The Sanders Family back together again to sing me out...And sing Dennis in! And would you look at this crowd! The parking lot full and cars parked up and down the road! June and I just pulled right up to the door 'cause of her delicate condition.

(VERA starts to rise. JUNE signs as she says –)

JUNE. I'm fine.

PASTOR OGLETHORPE. *(Beaming with pride.)* She doesn't sing, she signs.

(JUNE stands and signs as she says –)

JUNE. I don't sing, I sign.

(JUNE begins to sign everything PASTOR OGLETHORPE says.)

PASTOR OGLETHORPE. I tell you, you never know what the Lord has planned. He'll just pick you up and shake you sometimes, won't he? Great things are on the horizon, but when our little caravan left the parsonage tonight, I admit it, I was feeling mighty low. The last few days I can't turn around without having to say goodbye. Goodbye to my home — Dennis, I promise, just a few little knickknacks and the parsonage is yours — goodbye to the pickle plant, goodbye to my first church, goodbye to my homeplace and my mama — *(JUNE sees where this is going and rallies her family to sing.)* I just felt like I had to go by the cemetery — *(Starting to choke up.)* — and say goodbye to Mama —

(As PASTOR OGLETHORPE starts to crack, VERA loudly plays the opening chord of the first song. JUNE ushers PASTOR OGLETHORPE to a pew.)

Song: *LEANING ON THE EVERLASTING ARMS*

THE SANDERS FAMILY.
WHAT A FELLOWSHIP,
WHAT A JOY DIVINE,
LEANING ON THE EVERLASTING ARMS;
WHAT A BLESSEDNESS,
WHAT A PEACE IS MINE,
LEANING ON THE EVERLASTING ARMS.
LEANING, LEANING,
SAFE AND SECURE FROM ALL ALARMS;
(JUNE strikes a triangle.)
LEANING, LEANING,
LEANING ON THE EVERLASTING ARMS.

(As the song ends, PASTOR OGLETHORPE attempts to rise from the pew. It's very difficult — he's having a rough sympathetic pregnancy. He sits back down as the SANDERS sing again.)

Song: GLORYLAND BOOGIE

THE SANDERS FAMILY.
THERE'S GONNA BE A MIGHTY LOT OF SINGING,
GONNA BE A MIGHTY LOT OF SHOUTING,
GONNA BE A LOT OF HALLELUJAHS
YONDER IN THE GLORYLAND.
OH, THERE'S GONNA BE A MIGHTY CHORUS
SINGING 'ROUND THE THRONE OF MY REDEEMER;
THERE'S GONNA BE A LOT OF SHOUTING
YONDER IN THE GLORYLAND.

STANLEY.
LITTLE DAVID, HE'S GONNA HAVE A HARP;
OL' GABRIEL WILL HAVE HIS HORN;
TEN THOUSAND THOUSAND SAINTS WILL SING

ON THE MIGHTY JUDGMENT MORN;
HALLELUJAH, GLORY TO THE LORD;
I'M A-HOLDING TO HIS HAND;
'CAUSE I KNOW THERE'S A-GONNA BE A MIGHTY
    MIGHTY SINGING
YONDER IN THE GLORY LAND

BURL. We are the Sanders Family Singers from up around Siler City. I'm Burl. Standing here slapping the bass is my brother Stanley, just come back to us.
STANLEY. Pleased to be here.
BURL. And on the piano is my wife Vera.

VERA.
LITTLE DAVID AIN'T A-GONNA PLAY HIS HARP,
OL' GABRIEL WON'T BLOW HIS HORN
'TIL THE GREAT CONDUCTOR OF US ALL
GIVES A SIGNAL ON THAT MORN;
THEN ALL THE SAINTS IN CHRIST SHALL RISE;
I WANT TO BE IN THAT BAND
'CAUSE I KNOW THERE'S GONNA BE A MIGHTY MIGHTY
    SINGING
YONDER IN THE GLORYLAND.

BURL. And these are my twins. Denise — she's the girl.
DENISE. Thank y'all for having us.
BURL. And Dennis is the boy.

(DENNIS shakes his head. DENISE pokes him in the ribs.)

DENNIS. Thank y'all.
DENISE. *(Gesturing toward the door.)* And *my* twins Weldon and Eldon!

DENNIS & DENISE.
I WANT TO BE THERE IN THAT HAPPY VALE
WHEN DAVID STARTS THAT CHORD.
I WANT TO HEAR OL' GABRIEL BLOW HIS HORN
IN PRAISES TO THE LORD;

I WANT TO HEAR OL' PAUL AND SILAS SING
THERE IN THAT HAPPY BAND;
YES, I KNOW THERE'S GONNA BE A MIGHTY MIGHTY
 SINGING
YONDER IN THE GLORYLAND.

 THE SANDERS FAMILY.
OH LORD, SOMEDAY I WANT TO GO TO GLORY
TO BE WITH THOSE I LOVE;
I KNOW THERE'LL BE A LOT OF FRIENDS AND NEIGHBORS
YONDER IN GLORYLAND;
WELL, AH, OH YES!
THERE'S GONNA BE A MIGHTY LOT OF SINGING,
GONNA BE A MIGHTY LOT OF SHOUTING,
GONNA BE A LOT OF HALLELUJAHS
YONDER IN THE GLORYLAND.
OH, THERE'S GONNA BE A MIGHTY CHORUS
SINGING 'ROUND THE THRONE OF MY REDEEMER;
THERE'S GONNA BE A LOT OF SHOUTING
YONDER IN THE GLORYLAND.

 BURL. And playing the devil out of that tambourine is my eldest, June.
 PASTOR OGLETHORPE. My Mrs. Oglethorpe!

 THE SANDERS FAMILY.
THERE'S GONNA BE A MIGHTY LOT OF SINGING,
GONNA BE A MIGHTY LOT OF SHOUTING,
GONNA BE A LOT OF HALLELUJAHS
YONDER IN THE GLORYLAND.
OH, THERE'S GONNA BE A MIGHTY CHORUS
SINGING 'ROUND THE THRONE OF MY REDEEMER;
THERE'S GONNA BE A LOT OF SHOUTING
YONDER IN THE GLORYLAND.

 BURL. The Sanders Family!

 THE SANDERS FAMILY.
YONDER IN GLORYLAND.

(After the song, PASTOR OGLETHORPE leads the congregation in applause.)

PASTOR OGLETHORPE. Yes! Praise the Lord! We're gonna raise the roof tonight!

BURL. The Sanders Family has been singing gospel for over forty years. Back in the beginning, it was just Mama, my brother Stanley, and me. We'd sing revivals, protracted meetings, brush arbors.

VERA. The state-wides —

BURL. Yes, ma'am. We got to thinking so much of ourselves we entered the state-wides in 1923.

VERA. They were good.

BURL. But we got way better after I poached Vera here from the Thistlethorne Sisters. Now, those were some singing girls. Vera and Mama had some trouble finding their harmonies in the beginning — *(VERA just smiles.)* — but sure enough, after Vera and me got married, the Sanders Family Singers started winning.

VERA. Even in Raleigh.

BURL. Young'uns didn't slow us up, no sir. We'd pile these children on top of the guitars and banjos and ride all over these mountains.

VERA. On long trips, I'd swaddle up the twins and put them down in the bass fiddle case.

BURL. No better cradle. But then Mama got so stove up she couldn't ride in the bus anymore. And we lost Stanley...to other interests. We had to give it up for, what, four years?

STANLEY. Five.

BURL. Then our dear mother was called on to Paradise.

PASTOR OGLETHORPE. Bless her heart. Mine, too.

BURL. But with Mama passing, the Sanders started back on the Gospel Circuit right here at Mount Pleasant Baptist Church. Oh, and that was the beginning of a big time. Picking and singing in the churches, on the radio, on phonograph albums.

VERA. We got fan mail!

BURL. But when the war started up, it just scattered the family like shot. My boy Dennis joined up and was shipped to the Pacific. Stanley took off back west. My baby girls got married and started having babies of their own. Thank God for this night. Thank

God for the blessing to be together one last time before we scatter for good. *(The SANDERS start to gather.)* We couldn't ask for a better Homecoming. The good Lord has seen fit to send Dennis and all our boys home to us. My girls are here and grown-up with good men of their own. My strong and steady wife by my side. And lo and behold, sittin' right out there on the back steps this evenin' like we'd ordered him up, my brother Stanley gone from us…oh, for way too long. And by God's good grace, I get to squeeze them all tight to me one last time. Call it for me, Mother.

VERA. "Although I have scattered them among the countries, yet will I be to them as a little sanctuary."

THE SANDERS FAMILY. Ezekiel 11:16.

BURL. Reverend Oglethorpe, how 'bout if we do "Everything You'll Need"?

PASTOR OGLETHORPE. Oh!

BURL. The preacher had us practicing this all day yesterday as we loaded the car. You ready?

PASTOR OGLETHORPE. I was ready yesterday!

Song: *EVERYTHING YOU'LL NEED*

THE SANDERS FAMILY.
IF YOU ARE SEARCHING FOR SWEET PEACE

PASTOR OGLETHORPE.
FOR PEACE WITHIN YOUR SOUL,

THE SANDERS FAMILY.
I HAVE GOOD NEWS

PASTOR OGLETHORPE.
I HAVE GOOD NEWS

THE SANDERS FAMILY & PASTOR OGLETHORPE.
FOR YOU;

THE SANDERS FAMILY.
THERE IS A SAVIOR, IF YOU GIVE

PASTOR OGLETHORPE.
IF YOU GIVE TO HIM CONTROL,

THE SANDERS FAMILY.
HIS WONDROUS GRACE

PASTOR OGLETHORPE.
HIS WONDROUS GRACE

THE SANDERS FAMILY & PASTOR OGLETHORPE.
WILL BRING YOU THROUGH.

THE SANDERS FAMILY.
EVERYTHING

PASTOR OGLETHORPE.
EVERYTHING YOU'LL EVER NEED,

THE SANDERS FAMILY.
YOU'LL FIND IN JESUS

PASTOR OGLETHORPE.
YOU'LL FIND IT IN JESUS CHRIST;

THE SANDERS FAMILY.
EVERYTHING

PASTOR OGLETHORPE.
EVERYTHING YOUR SOUL DESIRES

THE SANDERS FAMILY & PASTOR OGLETHORPE.
HE SATISFIES; HE WILL MAKE FOR YOU A WAY
FOR HE KNOWS YOUR NEED BEFORE YOU PRAY;
EVERYTHING YOU NEED YOU'LL FIND IN MY LORD.

THE SANDERS FAMILY.
THERE IS A FOUNTAIN ALWAYS FULL

PASTOR OGLETHORPE.
THAT NEVER SHALL RUN DRY;

THE SANDERS FAMILY & PASTOR OGLETHORPE.
IT COMES FROM CALV'RY'S FLOW;

THE SANDERS FAMILY.
MILLIONS HAVE TASTED AND RECEIVED ·

PASTOR OGLETHORPE.
AND RECEIVED HIS LIFE ANEW;

THE SANDERS FAMILY.
AND YOU'LL FIND

PASTOR OGLETHORPE.
YOU'LL FIND SUFFICIENT

THE SANDERS FAMILY & PASTOR OGLETHORPE.
GRACE, I KNOW.

THE SANDERS FAMILY.
EVERYTHING

PASTOR OGLETHORPE.
EVERYTHING YOU'LL EVER NEED,

THE SANDERS FAMILY.
YOU'LL FIND IN JESUS

PASTOR OGLETHORPE.
YOU'LL FIND IT IN JESUS CHRIST;

THE SANDERS FAMILY.
EVERYTHING

PASTOR OGLETHORPE.
EVERYTHING YOUR SOUL DESIRES

THE SANDERS FAMILY & PASTOR OGLETHORPE.
HE SATISFIES;
HE WILL MAKE FOR YOU A WAY
FOR HE KNOWS YOUR NEED BEFORE YOU PRAY;
EVERYTHING YOU NEED YOU'LL FIND IN MY LORD.
HE WILL MAKE FOR YOU A WAY
FOR HE KNOWS YOUR NEED BEFORE YOU PRAY;
EVERYTHING YOU NEED YOU'LL FIND

PASTOR OGLETHORPE.
IN MY LORD

THE SANDERS FAMILY.
IN MY LORD.

PASTOR OGLETHORPE. Praise the Lord! As Preacher, Choir Director, Chairman of Finance, Director of Education, and Youth Director, I'd like to welcome you all to Mount Pleasant Baptist Church and thank you for sharing your beautiful voices with us tonight.

THE SANDERS FAMILY. You're welcome.

VERA. "Sing forth the honor of His name. Make His praise glorious — "

PASTOR OGLETHORPE. — Psalms 66:2. Amen, thank you, Mrs. Sanders. And nothing gives me more joy than to know we are all standing here working for one thing. Getting right with Jesus in song and revelation.

THE SANDERS FAMILY. Amen.

PASTOR OGLETHORPE. A special greeting to all you folks from the Loudsville Church of God, Kettle Rock Fire-Baptized Holiness, and the Two-Seed-in-the-Spirit Predestinarian Baptist. The doors of Mount Pleasant swing on welcome hinges. And sitting over there in the Amen Corner next to Miss Maude and Miss Myrtle — Miss Maude, Miss Myrtle, thank you again for the beautiful...

(He looks at JUNE.)

JUNE. Layette set.

PASTOR OGLETHORPE. Layette set. But sitting next to Miss Maude and Miss Myrtle is our new friend Preacher Clyde Nations, Sr. with his son Clyde, Jr. Miss Maude and Miss Myrtle invited Reverend Nations up to help me with our revival and foot-washing this past August. And I tell you, nobody tells the old, old story of Jesus and His love like Brother Clyde. Fifteen souls were washed clean and purified in one week. And Clyde, Jr. coming up in his daddy's footsteps. I haven't had the privilege of hearing you preach, Clyde, Jr., but Miss Maude and Miss Myrtle say it's like fire going through the broomstraw. That's wonderful. A wonderful gift. Dennis, you're going to be seeing a lot more of Clyde, Jr. if these dear ladies have anything to say about it. *(To congregation.)* And thank you all so much for this fine send-off. Tomorrow afternoon, Mrs. Oglethorpe and I set off on the adventure of our lifetimes. The Lord has called me to preach in Wildorado, Texas. And from the look of the map, it's about as far west in Texas as you can get. I'm gonna ride the range and herd up souls for Jesus! Lasso me some sinners! *(PASTOR OGLETHORPE laughs. VERA starts to rise.)* But this has not been a light calling for me. The good folks of Wildorado approached me at the Missionary Meeting in Atlanta this summer. I preached a little sermonette, and I guess it went over all right. The Texas people seemed to think a lot of it. Said right up front they wanted me to come out West. Said they built a little church out there amongst the dry gulches and tumbleweeds and it's standing there plumb empty for lack of a preacher. And they're starving to hear the gospel! It meant the world to me that they asked, but I said, "I've got a new wife and my first child is on the way. I best stay put." Drove back to Mount Pleasant. Thought I was done with it. But it burdened me. I couldn't get my mind off those folks' open hearts and true need. And I prayed on it.

You all know I bookkeep part-time down at the Mount Pleasant Pickle Plant. And thank you good women from the second shift so much for the tiny bootie and hat sets y'all crocheted. I can't believe a foot could be that small, but June says it better be. *(VERA looks to JUNE. JUNE mouths and signs, "I'm fine.")* Anyway, I was sitting at my desk running the adding machine and having a few spicy dills when the burden came over my heart so hard I thought it was going to bust. Norma McKeever, who sits right next to me, asked if I'd caught a red pepper flake, and I just let loose crying and carrying on. I told her I'd been praying and worrying on it so hard, but the Lord wasn't sending me an answer. And Norma said, "Mervin, if you want your prayers to get beyond the ceiling, you have to listen when God speaks." And those few words dried me right up. And I took it to the Lord real quiet-like, and the Lord opened the way. If Jesus can go out to the wilderness, so can I. These here mountains used to be just like Texas! Wilderness! 'Til Daniel Boone came through here and tamed us! I'm gonna be a Daniel Boone for the Lord! Wildorado! Muleshoe! Horsehead Crossing! I've only seen pictures. It looks a little sparse and lonesome, but full of opportunities. It's the Wild Wild West! I'll be gunslinging for the Lord!

(VERA starts to rise again.)

    BURL. Mother.
    PASTOR OGLETHORPE. But I will miss you all so much. Yesterday was my last reconcile at Pleasant Pickles. And Norma made my favorite — Ten Commandments Cake with ten candles, one for each "Thou shalt not". Mr. Dexter Callahan, president of Pleasant Pickles, came out to shake my hand and gifted me with a whole case of extra-fancy gherkins. *(He starts to choke up.)* I don't know why, but I can't get enough pickle these days.

(JUNE stands and raises her hand.)

    JUNE. Time to sing!

(The others scramble for the instruments before PASTOR
    OGLETHORPE breaks down.)

Song: *I'LL NEVER DIE*

THE SANDERS FAMILY & PASTOR OGLETHORPE.

ON THAT GREAT TRIUMPHANT MORNING
IN THE TWINKLING OF AN EYE,
THE SAINTS WILL ALL BE GATHERED
UP YONDER IN THE SKY;
ALL THE GRAVES WILL BREAK OPEN
AND THE LIVING THEN SHALL RISE

AND GO TO LIVE WITH JESUS
UP YONDER IN THE SKIES.
IN JUST A FLEETING MOMENT
WHEN THE TRUMP SHALL SOUND
I WILL FLY, FLY, FLY, FLY UP TO THE SKY.
THERE I'LL LIVE WITH JESUS WHILE THE YEARS ROLL
    BY;
WITH MY LORD, WITH MY LORD, WITH MY LORD, WITH
    MY LORD,
THERE I'LL NEVER DIE.
THERE'LL BE NO GRAVE TO HOLD ME
WHEN I GO BEYOND THE SKY;
MY BLESSED LORD WILL MEET ME
AND FLY BY MY SIDE;
ANGELS WILL BE REJOICING
FOR THE BRIDE IS NOW AT HOME;
WE'LL LIVE UP THERE FOREVER
AND NEVER, NEVER ROAM.
IN JUST A FLEETING MOMENT
WHEN THE TRUMP SHALL SOUND
I WILL FLY, FLY, FLY, FLY UP TO THE SKY.
THERE I'LL LIVE WITH JESUS WHILE THE YEARS ROLL
    BY;
WITH MY LORD, WITH MY LORD, WITH MY LORD, WITH
    MY LORD,
THERE I'LL NEVER DIE.
WITH MY LORD, WITH MY LORD, WITH MY LORD, WITH
    MY LORD,
THERE I'LL NEVER DIE.
I'LL NEVER DIE.

PASTOR OGLETHORPE. Yes! We are walking temples of song! Now, before we get carried away with the spirit, I want us to take a minute to remember those in our flock who could not be with us tonight. *(He pulls out a little card from his pocket.)* Please join our prayer chain for Miss Elzie Peast, down with the bursitis, arthritis, they don't know what all. Elzie's so frustrated she thinks they're apt to name a disease after her.

    BURL. Bless her heart.

PASTOR OGLETHORPE. Chunk Lloyd's bowel has seized up on him again. It's chronic. And Tolliver Vinson called me on the telephone — Dennis, I told you you're on a five-party line out there, didn't I?

DENNIS. You told me.

PASTOR OGLETHORPE. Just listen for a second before dialing. The ladies out there like to go over what they heard on last night's radio shows of an afternoon. "The Guiding Light" is getting so good, sometimes I join in!

DENNIS. I will.

PASTOR OGLETHORPE. Well, Tolliver called to say his kidney stone has finally passed after a month of suffering.

BURL. Lord have mercy.

PASTOR OGLETHORPE. It was a stubborn one. Said it made him yip a bit, but he was thankful to be shed of it.

THE SANDERS FAMILY. Amen.

PASTOR OGLETHORPE. And thank you all for your prayers on mine and June's coming addition. And for all the nice baby gifts and name suggestions. We've decided Mervin, Jr. if it's a boy. And if it's a girl, well, of course, we'll name her after my Mama.

JUNE. Narvelia.

STANLEY. Pray for a boy.

PASTOR OGLETHORPE. But the way these Sanders women go, I wouldn't be surprised if it was twins or — look at the way she's puffed out — triplets!

JUNE. I'm not having triplets.

PASTOR OGLETHORPE. We're figuring about three weeks, isn't that right, June?

JUNE. *(Signing)* Two.

PASTOR OGLETHORPE. Two! *(Gesturing to the pink suitcase beside the pulpit.)* But we've got our little case ready for the hospital. I know it sounds a little fool-hardy to take off for parts unknown at such a time, but June swears she can hold it. *(JUNE gives an "OK" sign.)* She's been a real trouper through all of this. Having a baby hasn't slowed her down one bit. I myself have not been right for months now. One minute I'm burning hot, then I'm icy cold, then my back's all out of whack —

BURL. Mother —

PASTOR OGLETHORPE. — my ankles are all swole up —
BURL. Mother —
VERA. You know, Pastor Oglethorpe, I wouldn't be surprised if June did have twins.
PASTOR OGLETHORPE. Really?
JUNE. I'm not having twins.
VERA. I'm not only the mother of twins, I'm the grandmother of twins. Weldon and Eldon Culpepper. And I know I'm partial, but they are just as adorable and smart as whips as Dennis and Denise were.

(DENISE perks up and runs to the door. She waves and whispers.)

DENISE. Donnie!

(Much gesturing as DENISE directs her husband.)

VERA. When my twins were just little bitty, we would dress them up and run them onstage for a specialty song.

(DENISE gets a tiny piano and places it front and center. She sets a small bell on it.)

DENISE. And folks ate us up with a spoon. *(DENISE pulls out two sparkly bowties on elastic and shows the congregation how adorable they are.)* It was one of the highlights of our sings.

(She heads out the door to retrieve her children.)

VERA. And from what I hear, these two little boys have been practicing up a storm to do one of the songs these twins and June did all those years ago. *(Everyone stands at the ready for DENISE and the twins to ENTER. Long pause.)* They're very musical boys. *(Pause.)* They're three years old...
BURL. ...They were born on Stanley's birthday.
STANLEY. Is that right?

(VERA shoots them all a look. DENNIS and JUNE share a look and almost start laughing at Denise's predicament. Pause.)

VERA. Denise made their little outfits herself —

(DENISE, all smiles, glides through the door, walks over to DEN-NIS, and tries to squeeze the bowtie over his head. It will only go down to his forehead. DENISE puts the other bowtie over her forehead and drags DENNIS toward the tiny piano. Apparently, WELDON and ELDON are no-shows.)

Song: *THE ROYAL TELEPHONE*

DENNIS & DENISE.
CENTRAL'S NEVER "BUSY," ALWAYS ON THE LINE;
YOU MAY HEAR FROM HEAVEN ALMOST ANY TIME;
'TIS A ROYAL SERVICE, FREE FOR ONE AND ALL;
WHEN YOU GET IN TROUBLE, GIVE THIS ROYAL LINE A CALL.

(It's almost time for JUNE's part. She tries kneeling down behind the piano in various ways. Unconsciously, the family mirrors her movements. Finally, she decides to just throw herself down on her knees. STANLEY slips his coat under her just as she's about to touch the floor.)

DENNIS & DENISE. *(CONT'D)*
TELEPHONE TO GLORY, OH, WHAT JOY DIVINE!

(JUNE rings the bell.)

I CAN FEEL THE CURRENT MOVING ON THE LINE,
BUILT BY GOD THE FATHER FOR HIS LOVED AND OWN,
WE MAY TALK TO JESUS ON THE ROYAL TELEPHONE.

DENISE.
FAIL TO GET THE ANSWER, SATAN'S CROSSED YOUR WIRE,
BY SOME STRONG DELUSION, OR SOME BASE DESIRE;

DENNIS.
PRAYER AND FAITH AND PROMISE MEND THE BROKEN

WIRE,
'TIL YOUR SOUL IS BURNING WITH THE PENTECOSTAL
FIRE.

(In the first chorus, JUNE only had to ring the bell, but now her job gets more complicated — she has to reach around DENNIS and DENISE, alternately hitting bass and treble notes. And she has to keep ringing that bell.)

DENNIS & DENISE.
TELEPHONE TO GLORY, OH, WHAT JOY DIVINE!
I CAN FEEL THE CURRENT MOVING ON THE LINE,
BUILT BY GOD THE FATHER FOR HIS LOVED AND OWN,
WE MAY TALK TO JESUS ON THE ROYAL TELEPHONE.

(DENNIS and DENISE, a devilish gleam in their eyes, repeat the chorus, speeding it up. This is a trick they used to pull on JUNE when they were children.)

DENNIS & DENISE. *(CONT'D)*
(Faster)
TELEPHONE TO GLORY, OH, WHAT JOY DIVINE!
I CAN FEEL THE CURRENT MOVING ON THE LINE,
BUILT BY GOD THE FATHER FOR HIS LOVED AND OWN,
WE MAY TALK TO JESUS ON THE ROYAL TELEPHONE.
(Even faster.)
WE MAY TALK TO JESUS ON THE
WE MAY TALK TO JESUS ON THE
WE MAY TALK TO JESUS ON THE ROYAL TELEPHONE.

(At the end of the song, VERA beams and almost asphyxiates DENNIS with a hug.)

BURL. I would not trade these twins of mine for anything.

(JUNE tries to get up, but can't.)

JUNE. Help me.

(Everyone rushes to help JUNE up.)

BURL. They're full of ginger, ain't they?
PASTOR OGLETHORPE. June?
JUNE. I'm fine.

(PASTOR OGLETHORPE settles JUNE onto a bench.)

BURL. When the Sanders Family wasn't singing, we'd run a little filling station-grocerette down on Highway 11 out near Siler City. That little store was sure good to us. We had folks humming in and out of there from morning 'til dark. Didn't matter if you wanted a bag of peanuts or the block rebuilt on your Buick, we were happy to serve.
PASTOR OGLETHORPE. Dennis is a fine mechanic.
BURL. The best, but I lost my mechanic to the United States Marines Corps.
VERA. And the ministry.
BURL. That rationing cooled off my business right smart. Then my cashiers ran off and got married.
DENISE. Daddy.
BURL. It's true. But I knew if I'd just be patient, our boys would beat the tar out of 'em over there, the war would end, and we'd bloom back up big again.
VERA. But then the mail came.
BURL. Yes, ma'am. The mail came! I remember it clear 'cause I was about to eat my sandwich. You know the only good thing that came out of this war was...
THE SANDERS FAMILY. Spam.
BURL. Spam. Make fun if you want, but when the good Lord inspired Hormel to mash whatever that all is into a loaf and give it a key, it was a blessing to me. Fried Spam on two pieces of Sunbeam bread with some of that good Pleasant Pickle mustard relish.
VERA. And Pleasant Pickle bread-and-butters on the side.
PASTOR OGLETHORPE. My mouth's watering.
BURL. Ain't it? So I'm enjoying my sandwich and rifling through the bills and whatnot, and there's a letter from the government. The United States of America big as day on the return

address. I pull out my buck knife and slide it across the top. And the first few lines cut me to the quick.

VERA. We're poor!

BURL. Somebody named Harvey Williams was writing to tell me I was poor. I had no idea. *(Grumbling from the SANDERs.)* Well, it's true the Sanders didn't have much to do with money 'til we got the filling station. Mama moved us to old man Pickard's place after Daddy left us. Paid our rent in tobacco and corn. I look back on it now, and I don't know how Mama did it, do you, Stanley?

STANLEY. Not hardly.

PASTOR OGLETHORPE. A mama is a powerful thing.

THE SANDERS FAMILY. Amen.

BURL. And Mama wouldn't let us sing for pay. Preachers would offer us an envelope, but Mama always said —

BURL & STANLEY. "Keep your money. We make our living at home."

BURL. Which don't mean we ever left empty-handed.

THE SANDERS FAMILY. Good gracious, no.

BURL. That just goes against church folks' natures. You're gonna take something home — something good.

VERA. A bushel of green tomatoes.

STANLEY. Smoked ham.

DENNIS. Rufus.

BURL. Every old dog or cat we had on the place came from one sing or the other.

VERA. The letter.

BURL. So this letter from Harvey Williams goes on to say that the government is contacting citizens of Chatham County residing on leased land and inviting them to participate in a low-interest farmland acquisition program. Translated, that means I can get a mortgage for practically nothing and own outright the farm my Mama had rented for fifty years. The dirt we had plowed and chopped and sweat on for so long could finally be ours. *(Beat)* This was the devil's work. I tore that paper up and threw it in the stove. I watched my mama work herself to death paying back the money my daddy owed. Washing other people's clothes, priming other people's tobacco. Stanley and me running up and down the ditches looking for Co-Cola bottles we can cash in for a penny. Raise up a big hog, sell the good meat, and we eat fatback and biscuits all winter. The taste of debt never leaves your mouth.

THE SANDERS FAMILY. Amen.

BURL. Yes, owning that farm would be nice, and Vera here was quick to point out that we'd done well enough with the filling station and our phonograph albums, we could have bought it a long time ago. But if it comes with a payment book, no thank you.

Months go by. I don't think anything more about it. Then about this time last year, I got the exact same letter offering the exact same terms. Nothing down, one percent interest. And there is nothing prettier than that farm in October. The leaves turning gold and red. The corn is laid by and the fodder is cut. That big blue sky.

Proverbs 22:26, "Don't be a man who strikes hands in pledge. If you cannot pay, your very bed will be snatched up from under you." I have borrowed money one time and one time only for —

(VERA has heard this a thousand times.)

BURL & VERA. Vera's back porch —

BURL. — and the worry of it about killed me. Let one thing set you back, and you're layin' bug-eyed in the bed fretting over what you can sell to get the money to satisfy the bank for the money they lent you for something you didn't need in the first place. I tore the letter up and threw it in the stove.

December. Devil in the mailbox. Why won't this Harvey Williams let me be? That farm at Christmastime. The grass crunching under your feet. The mule and the cows wearing their furry winter coats. Walking the fence with my family, looking for the perfect tree. I let the letter linger on the mantel. Then I tore it up and threw it in the stove. 'Round about the middle of March, I'm sitting in the filling station, and a young boy no older than Dennis walks in. Says he's Harvey Williams out from Pittsboro and he's come to encourage me to become part of the government land program. I told him I had considered it and thought I better not. He shows me how he's worked it out on paper. I was a little put out that this government boy knew so much about my private finances. I said I'd weighed the aughts and the naughts and believed I better naught. Harvey Williams said the government wouldn't ask if they didn't think I could do it. "You can do it, Mr. Sanders." I didn't want to get ugly with the fella, but how many times does a man have to say no?

"You can do this, Mr. Sanders. We're closing the books on it March thirty-first." I told him I'd hang the matter on a hook for further consideration. "I look forward to hearing from you, Mr. Sanders." I was so mad I about pawed the floor.

'Cause it was spring. And I love that farm in the spring. The baby chicks, the buttercups, the fresh-plowed dirt. This is the house I grew up in. This is the house I brought my wife to, where my children were born, where my mama died. I knew I was done for when I started getting teary about the outhouse.

I sat that afternoon and filled out every form, signed and initialled and swore and oathed. Walked that big envelope down to the mailbox. I looked back up the road at the house and the barn. No more beautiful sight. I slammed the door and put up the flag.

March twenty-seventh. *(BURL shakes his head.)* I've never seen anything like it. You remember. Turned off bitter cold about dark and then started pouring rain. I knew we were in trouble when branches started breaking in the night. Loud as gunshots. Remember sunrise that morning? Ice thick as your thumb covering everything. No water, no electricity, no radio, no telephone. And it just got colder. On the third morning of it, I'm trying to get to the pigpen when something pulls my eye down towards the road. [That red flag. Frozen straight up.] The deadline is March thirty-first. Today is March thirty-first. *(Beat)* I have to walk to Pittsboro. I tied burlap sacks to my brogans for traction. Got me two shovel handles for balance. Vera offers up that it's eight miles to Pittsboro.

That the road's too slick to walk. I'm going to fall in a ditch and break my neck. And that I was nothing but a bull-headed, half-cocked, stubborn fool. "Hurry," she said. I made a good show of it. Walk two steps, wham, fall. Slide two steps, wham, fall. The ice stuck to my overalls and wet me to the bone. My elbows and knees were bloody, and I'd gone no more than a mile. But I kept walking. I bargained with the Lord and shouted back to the Devil. And then I thought about Mama, and nothing could keep me from pushing on through.

I limped to the courthouse about four o'clock. Not a car in sight. I pushed open the door and looked around. Nobody. Nothing but echo. I'd have cried if I weren't so cold. I'd come all this way for nothing. I started out the door to crawl back home. Then I figure I'll find where Harvey Williams sits, leave my envelope on his desk, maybe it'll count. Directory says Room 203. I walk down the hall. 201, 202, Room 203. And sitting there scribbling away in Room 203 is Harvey Williams. I said, "Lord, boy, what are you doing here?" And Harvey Williams looks up and smiles real big and says, "I've been waiting for you."

A truck spreading salt picked me up on the way home. Sitting in the cab I considered Harvey Williams and all he had done for me. And I thought, isn't that the way with the Lord? Our Savior gives us opportunity after opportunity after opportunity. And our fear and our pride and our self-glory keeps us from Him. 'Til finally we wear down and open our hearts and say, "Take me, Lord." And He spreads His arms wide and he says, "I've been waiting for you."

THE SANDERS FAMILY & PASTOR OGLETHORPE. Amen.

BURL. So here Vera and I are, grandma and grandpa, and we agree to become full-time farmers. I admit I carved a little sign - Sanders Family Farm , Established 1945 — tacked it out there. Horace Ward and his family have taken up the filling station. He's got two boys just back from Germany. They can tear a car down and put it back together in five minutes. Y'all stop by there and see them. Me and Vera will be busy pulling tobacco worms off the tomatoes. Romans 13:8 — call it for me, Mother —

VERA. "Pay all your debts except the debt of love for others. Never finish paying that."

Song: *A LITTLE AT A TIME*

BURL.
FROM THE MOMENT THAT I GET UP TILL THE TIME I GO
    TO BED,
LORD, I JUST KEEP SEARCHING FOR A WAY TO GET
    AHEAD;
I'M ON A NARROW HIGHWAY;
LORD, I'M DOING FINE AS I MAKE MY WAY TO HEAVEN

BURL, VERA & STANLEY.
A LITTLE AT A TIME, A LITTLE AT A TIME.

BURL.
THERE'S WORKERS NEEDING SUNSHINE, FARMERS
    NEEDING RAIN,
FIELDS THAT NEED A-PLANTING 'CAUSE THE CATTLE
    NEED THE GRAIN;
I NEED A LITTLE SHOVE, LORD; I'M GETTING WAY
    BEHIND,
BUT, LORD, I'M GONNA CATCH UP

BURL, VERA & STANLEY.
A LITTLE AT A TIME, A LITTLE AT A TIME.

BURL.
I AIN'T GOT MUCH DOWN HERE, LORD, BUT I DO THE
    BEST I CAN,
AND WHEN I GET TO GLORY, I'M GONNA BE A WEALTHY
    MAN;
I'LL BE LIVING IN A MANSION, AND I WON'T OWE A DIME;
I'M LAYING UP MY TREASURES THERE

BURL, VERA & STANLEY.
A LITTLE AT A TIME, A LITTLE AT A TIME.

BURL.
I'M LAYING UP MY TREASURES THERE

BURL, VERA & STANLEY.
A LITTLE AT A TIME, A LITTLE AT A TIME.

    PASTOR OGLETHORPE. Thank you, Burl. And thank you for your witness.
    BURL. Well, Brother Oglethorpe, the Sanders Family believes that witnessing is the most important part of our ministry.
    VERA. That's right, Mervin — *(Bam! Something hits the side of the church.)* — We believe God has given us two gifts — *(Bam! DENISE scurries out the back door.)* — music and witness. *(Bam!)* What in the world?

(DENISE comes in.)

DENISE. They found a ball. Donnie and I would like to apologize to y'all for our twins hanging back from their song. You know how bashful three-year-olds can be. And June fed them something right before we left that didn't sit right in their little stomachs. June's not a mother yet so she doesn't understand tender tummies like real mommies do. *(Bam!)* But they're obviously feeling better — *(Bam!)* — and they've got their little outfits on and Donnie's bringing them in in a minute. *(DENISE runs out the door. Long beat. She comes back inside and stands by the piano.)* I'll sing.

Song: *CHILDREN TALK TO ANGELS*

DENISE.
CHILDREN TALK TO ANGELS, AT LEAST THAT'S WHAT
    THEY SAY;
CHILDREN TALK TO ANGELS ALMOST EVERY DAY;
BE CAREFUL WHEN YOU SCOLD THEM FOR THINGS
    THEY'LL LIKELY DO
'CAUSE CHILDREN TALK TO ANGELS LIKE THEY TALK TO
    ME AND YOU.

(JUNE rises and starts to sign.)

LISTEN, ALL YOU GROWNUPS WHO THINK YOU'RE BIG
    AND STRONG;
YOU MUST BECOME AS A LITTLE CHILD IN HEAVEN TO
    BELONG;
SO IF YOU PRAY TO JESUS LIKE LITTLE CHILDREN DO,
THEN YOU WILL UNDERSTAND THEM AND YOU'LL TALK
    TO ANGELS, TOO.
CHILDREN TALK TO ANGELS, AT LEAST THAT'S WHAT
    THEY SAY;
CHILDREN TALK TO ANGELS ALMOST EVERY DAY;
BE CAREFUL WHEN YOU SCOLD THEM FOR THINGS
    THEY'LL LIKELY DO
'CAUSE CHILDREN TALK TO ANGELS LIKE THEY TALK TO
    ME AND YOU.
YES, JESUS LOVES ME, YES, JESUS LOVES ME,
YES, JESUS LOVES ME, FOR THE BIBLE TELLS ME SO.

DENISE. *(Cont'd)* Dennis and I are twins. We went to Cullowhee Bible School. We cost too much to go together, so we traded years. Dennis graduated before me and joined the Marines. I determined to quit school and join the USO. But Mama said she hadn't done without all those years for me to throw it away doling out donuts and coffee to grabby Army boys.

I was furious about having to go back to school. Cullowhee Bible College might as well have been a girls' school once the war broke out. Every boy was drafted or enlisted. Something about June marrying Mervin just set a fire under me. Time was passing me by and I could see my future plain as day — a fussy old maid in a dowdy hat sitting in the Amen Corner. *(PASTOR OGLETHORPE looks to MISS MAUDE and MISS MYRTLE and practically passes out.)* But on the first day of the semester, standing right there in line for registration was the cutest 4-F you've ever laid your eyes on. Flat-footed, bifocals, a little knock-kneed. He wasn't going anywhere. Mama said I married the first thing I tripped over for spite.

VERA. We love Donnie.

DENISE. But, no. Donnie Culpepper said he's been waiting for me all his life. Donnie Culpepper of Culpepper Appliances — with two locations in Asheville, Hickory, and soon to open in Mount Pilot. And we are the proud parents of little Weldon and Eldon Culpepper. They got the Sanders head and the Culpepper body.

It was always understood that Donnie would join his daddy in the appliance business after graduation. And it's true, we did have Weldon and Eldon lickety-split 'cause June may have gotten married first, but nobody was gonna beat me to the first grandbaby. And twins! It was too perfect.

You all have to have noticed these hillsides around here sprouting houses like mushrooms. With all these GIs coming back, they can't build homes fast enough. And what does every one of those little houses need? Culpepper Appliances! And who better to sell a woman a washing machine than another woman? Daddy Culpepper didn't like the idea at all. Said I should stay home with the boys. But I said, "When Jesus took off through Galilee to spread the gospel, did he just take the twelve disciples?" No! He took women — Mary and Joanna and Susanna.

And I am a natural-born salesperson. I credit my excellent education and extensive performing background. Before I got married and became a mother, I planned to be a movie star. I auditioned for "Gone with the Wind" in Charlotte and almost got it.

But being a career woman and a mother took some adjusting. The children were so bright and inquisitive, it was hard to keep a babysitter. They used to stay at Mama and Daddy's, but they pulled up all of Mama's four-o-clocks *(To VERA.)* to make Mamaw a bouquet. And Daddy accused Weldon and Eldon of throwing his precious cat Valvoline down the well, but I think Valvoline jumped. That cat was always skittish. What kind of cat doesn't like to be chased?

So I set up a little playpen for them in the back of the appliance store. They've chewed through it a couple of times, but somebody always brings them back.

Mama used to say we children were sending her to an early grave. I find motherhood a blessing and, honestly, a breeze. And I do it alone! Shoot, Mama had Grandma Sanders and June to help her with Dennis and me. And no offense, Dennis, but I've read the baby books — we were just average compared to my boys - *(Bam!)* Weldon and Eldon are accelerated in every way — *(Bam!)* — mentally and physically — *(Bam!)* If the stores would just think — *(Bam!)* — my boys wouldn't have any problems — *(Bam!)* Don't put Evening in Paris bath powder on the bottom shelf, Mr. Woolworth — *(Bam!)* — if you don't want Evening in Paris bath powder all over your floors — *(Bam!)* What's a three-year-old supposed to do, Mr. Piggly-Wiggly — *(Bam!)* — when you put in a coffee grinder — *(Bam!)* — with a handle that just begs to be swung from? *(Bam!)* These are good children. *(No bam. Silence. It's over. DENISE breaks into a beaming smile.)* Darling children. Precious, darling, wonderful children. *(DENISE moves to the back door. Enormous crash! With her back still to the congregation, she begins to break down.)* I have prayed, repented, fasted, confessed, read my Bible —

VERA. Denise —

(DENISE walks toward the congregation.)

DENISE. — led prayer meetings, meditated reverently, pleaded fervently —
BURL. Honey —

DENISE. "Mama", "Mama", "Mama", "Mama", "Mama"!! *(She turns and goes out the back door.)* Donnie!!!

VERA. We love Donnie.

BURL. Donnie puts up with a lot. *(BURL starts playing the intro to the next song.)* Join us, Merv.

(PASTOR OGLETHORPE jumps right in, hoping to cover the fussing that can now be heard from outside. JUNE stands and begins to sign.)

Song: *STANDING ON THE PROMISES*

PASTOR OGLETHORPE.
STANDING ON THE PROMISES OF CHRIST MY KING,

PASTOR OGLETHORPE & BURL.
THROUGH ETERNAL AGES LET HIS PRAISES RING;

PASTOR OGLETHORPE, BURL, DENNIS, & STANLEY.
GLORY IN THE HIGHEST I WILL SHOUT AND SING,
STANDING ON THE PROMISES OF GOD.

(VERA has gone to the door and is looking out, concerned. From time to time, DENISE comes and cries on her mother's shoulder, then goes back to fuss at her children and husband.)

STANDING ON THE PROMISES, STANDING ON THE PROM-
ISES,
STANDING ON THE PROMISES OF GOD MY SAVIOR;
STANDING ON THE PROMISES, STANDING ON THE PROM-
ISES,
I'M STANDING ON THE PROMISES OF GOD.

(Every now and then, JUNE gets confused in her signing and inadvertently signs some of DENISE's fussing instead of the song lyrics.)

PASTOR OGLETHORPE.
STANDING ON THE PROMISES I CANNOT FALL,

LISTENING EVERY MOMENT TO THE SPIRIT'S CALL,
RESTING IN MY SAVIOR AS MY ALL IN ALL,

PASTOR OGLETHORPE, BURL, DENNIS, & STANLEY.
STANDING ON THE PROMISES OF GOD.

(DENISE comes back and sinks into a pew, weeping softly. She real-
izes the congregation's eyes are on her. She puts on a brave
smile and holds up a cute little outfit, which apparently got torn
off whichever twin it belonged to. She dabs her eyes with it.)

STANDING ON THE PROMISES, STANDING ON THE PROM-
        ISES,
STANDING ON THE PROMISES OF GOD MY SAVIOR;

STANDING ON THE PROMISES, STANDING ON THE PROM-
        ISES,
I'M STANDING ON THE PROMISES OF GOD.

VERA. Dennis.
DENNIS. Well, it wouldn't be a Saturday Night Sing at Mount
Pleasant if I didn't say, "My name is Dennis Sanders. I'm one of
the twins."
VERA. He's the boy.
DENNIS. "And I'm the boy." I used to hate saying that. But if
these last four years have taught me anything, it's to hang tight to
the things you can count on. My name is Dennis Sanders and I'm
one of the twins.
VERA. Dennis was a complete and total surprise!
DENNIS. And thanks to you good folks' vote of confidence,
I'm to be your new preacher. And I'll tell you, I'm more than a lit-
tle nervous about filling Brother Oglethorpe's shoes.
PASTOR OGLETHORPE. Oh, go on.
DENNIS. I feel like I grew up in the ministry right here at Mount
Pleasant. Reverend Oglethorpe was always quick to help a young boy
out. I'll never stand behind a pulpit with my feet just so and pick up the
Bible or raise a hand without thinking of you, Mervin. I once asked
Reverend Oglethorpe what a sermon should be about. He thought on it
a minute, then he said, "About God — "

PASTOR OGLETHORPE. "— and about ten minutes." Good advice.

DENNIS. When I was a young boy, I knew I had the conviction to preach, but deep in my heart, I was afraid serving the Lord was a soft thing best suited for women and children. I was wrong. There is no harder place on earth to fall to your knees and pray than a boot camp barracks. I wouldn't do it. But Jesse Jakes would. Every night, Jesse dropped to his knees and lifted up a prayer. And those boys who would call themselves leathernecks crowed. Threw shoes at his head. Told him in none too pretty language what he could do with his mumbling. But Jesse knelt beside his bunk and he prayed through.

Jesse had a little Bible his wife had given him that he kept in his left breast pocket. Any downtime, you'd see him leafing through. And the boys in the barracks would snatch that book and toss it from bunk to bunk 'til eventually it got back to the patient Jesse Jakes. Jesse refused to work on the Sabbath. Even KP. And it made the rest of the unit so mad some of them vowed when they went into combat, they'd shoot him themselves.

Last April, our unit was sent to Okinawa. Assigned to take the Maeda Escarpment. Nothing but sharp boulders and hill. A thirty-foot cliff at the top. We'd never seen artillery so fierce. Everybody not killed or wounded was driven back down. Except Jesse Jakes. Jesse refused to leave those torn-up boys behind. He crawled from soldier to soldier, fire flying over his head. Dragged them to the cliff and lowered them down on a litter rigged with rope by himself, boy by boy, to friendly hands. "Dear Lord," he kept saying. "Let me get just one more." He got close to fifty. I later asked those boys how they thought they survived and each to a one said, "Jesse Jakes prayed for me."

Two weeks later during a night attack, Jesse was looking after the wounded when a grenade exploded and shattered both his legs. When word got out that Jesse had lost his beloved pocket Bible in that night's battle, our outfit mobilized like nothing you've ever seen. We combed every inch of sand and rock, and miracle of miracles, somebody found that Bible. It was wet and muddy, but it was Jesse Jakes's all right. Those Marines careful-like brushed off the dirt and — easy — dried each thin page, flimsy as onion skin.

But it was too late. Jesse Jakes died on May twenty-third, five months ago. *(DENNIS pauses to collect himself.)* Paul wrote to Timothy that God did not give us a spirit of timidity, but a spirit of power and of love. You have to be tough to follow the Lord. The Reverend Oglethorpe puts a lot of stock in the Apostle Paul. And to tell the truth, I've always felt like his Timothy. Paul told Timothy to fight the good fight of faith. I want men everywhere to lift up holy hands in prayer. And we will fan into flame this gift of God. Great is the mystery of godliness —

PASTOR OGLETHORPE. Amen —

DENNIS. God was manifest in the flesh —

THE SANDERS FAMILY & PASTOR OGLETHORPE. Yes, he was —

DENNIS. Justified in the spirit —

THE SANDERS FAMILY & PASTOR OGLETHORPE. Yes, sir —

DENNIS. Seen by angels!

THE SANDERS FAMILY & PASTOR OGLETHORPE. Angels!

DENNIS. Preached unto nations!

THE SANDERS FAMILY & PASTOR OGLETHORPE. Nations!.

DENNIS. Believed on in this world!

THE SANDERS FAMILY & PASTOR OGLETHORPE. Oh, yes!

DENNIS. And received up into glory!

THE SANDERS FAMILY & PASTOR OGLETHORPE. Amen!

DENNIS. Let us praise Him.

(The family sings and JUNE signs the river medley.)

Song: *SHALL WE GATHER AT THE RIVER*

THE SANDERS FAMILY.
SHALL WE GATHER AT THE RIVER,
WHERE BRIGHT ANGEL FEET HAVE TROD,
WITH ITS CRYSTAL TIDE FOREVER
FLOWING BY THE THRONE OF GOD?
YES, WE'LL GATHER AT THE RIVER,

THE BEAUTIFUL, THE BEAUTIFUL RIVER;
GATHER WITH THE SAINTS AT THE RIVER
THAT FLOWS BY THE THRONE OF GOD.

Song: *I'M GOING TO CANAAN*

THE SANDERS FAMILY & PASTOR OGLETHORPE.
I'M GONNA CROSS OVER THE RIVER OF JORDAN,
AND WHEN I CROSS OVER, THEN I'LL TAKE MY SAVIOR'S
    HAND.
I'LL SING HALLELUJAH AS I CROSS THE RIVER
AND STEP INTO CANAAN, YES, I'M GOING TO THE
    CANAAN LAND.
I'M GOING TO CANAAN, I'M GOING TO CANAAN,
I'M GOING TO CANAAN, YES, I'M GOING TO THE CANAAN
    LAND.
I'M GONNA CROSS OVER THE RIVER OF JORDAN,
I'M GOING TO CANAAN, YES, I'M GOING TO THE CANAAN
    LAND.
I'M GOING TO CANAAN, I'M GOING TO CANAAN,
I'M GOING TO CANAAN, YES, I'M GOING TO THE CANAAN
    LAND.
I'M GONNA CROSS OVER THE RIVER OF JORDAN,
I'M GOING TO CANAAN, YES, I'M GOING TO THE CANAAN
    LAND.

Song: *YOU CAN SWIM*

THE SANDERS FAMILY.
OH, YOU CAN SWIM TO THE OTHER SHORE
EVEN IF YOU'VE NEVER BEEN IN DEEP WATER BEFORE;
JESUS WILL PROVIDE HIS SOUL-SAVING TIDE,
AND YOU CAN SWIM TO THE OTHER SHORE.

VERA & DENISE.
YOU MAY FLAIL AND FLOUNDER
AND PUMP YOUR LEGS IN VAIN;
KEEP YOUR HEAD ABOVE THE WATER,
AND TRY NOT TO COMPLAIN;

JUST RIDE THE SWELLS AND BILLOWS,
AND DO THE BEST YOU CAN;

THE SANDERS FAMILY.
AND GOD WILL GUIDE YOU TO HIS PROMISED LAND.

OH, YOU CAN SWIM TO THE OTHER SHORE
EVEN IF YOU'VE NEVER BEEN IN DEEP WATER BEFORE;
JESUS WILL PROVIDE HIS SOUL-SAVING TIDE,
AND YOU CAN SWIM TO THE OTHER SHORE.

BURL, DENNIS & STANLEY.
THERE'S STORMS UPON LIFE'S WATERS
NO MATTER WHERE YOU ROAM
AND UNDERTOWS AND DEADLY FLOWS
BENEATH THE RAGING FOAM;
AND IF A MIGHTY WHIRLPOOL
TURNS YOU UPSIDE DOWN,

THE SANDERS FAMILY.
JUST HOLD YOUR BREATH 'CAUSE GOD WON'T LET YOU
DROWN.

OH, YOU CAN SWIM TO THE OTHER SHORE
EVEN IF YOU'VE NEVER BEEN IN DEEP WATER BEFORE;
JESUS WILL PROVIDE HIS SOUL-SAVING TIDE,
AND YOU CAN SWIM TO THE OTHER SHORE.
YES, YOU CAN SWIM TO THE OTHER SHORE.

Song: *FAR SIDE BANKS OF JORDAN*

BURL.
I BELIEVE MY STEPS ARE GROWING WEARIER EACH DAY;
STILL I'VE GOT A JOURNEY ON MY MIND;
LURES OF THIS OLD WORLD HAVE CEASED TO MAKE ME
    WANT TO STAY,
AND MY ONE REGRET IS LEAVING YOU BEHIND.

VERA.
IF IT PROVES TO BE HIS WILL THAT I AM FIRST TO GO,
AND SOMEHOW I'VE A FEELING IT WILL BE,
WHEN IT COMES YOUR TIME TO TRAVEL LIKEWISE,
DON'T YOU FEEL LOST,
FOR I WILL BE THE FIRST ONE THAT YOU'LL SEE.

BURL & VERA.
AND I'LL BE WAITING ON THE FAR SIDE BANKS OF
    JORDAN;
I'LL BE WAITING, DRAWING PICTURES IN THE SAND;
AND WHEN I SEE YOU COMING, I WILL RISE UP WITH A
    SHOUT
AND COME RUNNING THROUGH THE SHALLOW WATERS
REACHING FOR YOUR HAND.

BURL.
THROUGH THIS LIFE WE LABOR HARD TO EARN OUR
    MEAGER FARE
'TWILL BRING US TREMBLING HANDS AND FAILING
    EYES.

VERA.
I'LL JUST REST HERE ON THIS SHORE AND TURN MY
    EYES AWAY
UNTIL YOU COME, THEN WE'LL SEE PARADISE.

BURL & VERA.
AND I'LL BE WAITING ON THE FAR SIDE BANKS OF
    JORDAN;
I'LL BE WAITING, DRAWING PICTURES IN THE SAND;
AND WHEN I SEE YOU COMING, I WILL RISE UP WITH A
    SHOUT
AND COME RUNNING THROUGH THE SHALLOW WATERS
REACHING FOR YOUR HAND.

THE SANDERS FAMILY.
AND I'LL BE WAITING ON THE FAR SIDE BANKS OF
    JORDAN;

I'LL BE WAITING DRAWING PICTURES IN THE SAND;
AND WHEN I SEE YOU COMING I WILL RISE UP WITH THE
  SHOUT
AND COME RUNNING THROUGH THE SHALLOW WATERS
REACHING FOR YOUR HAND.

BURL. We got this arrangement from our good friend Early
Upchurch in Mount Airy.

Song: *I AM READY TO GO*

THE SANDERS FAMILY.
IN THIS WORLD OF DOUBT AND SIN,
I AM READY NOW TO GO;
JESUS CAME AND TOOK ME IN;
I AM READY NOW TO GO.

*(During the song, PASTOR OGLETHORPE starts to choke up
  about leaving.)*

PASTOR OGLETHORPE. I'm sorry. I'm sorry. I'll just miss
you all so much...

THE SANDERS FAMILY.
I'M GETTING READY NOW
TO SAIL AWAY

PASTOR OGLETHORPE. Isn't this the nicest little church in
the world?...

THE SANDERS FAMILY.
TO THE MIGHTY HOME ON HIGH
WHERE I WILL EVER STAY;

PASTOR OGLETHORPE. And the best congregation...

THE SANDERS FAMILY.
UNTIL THE DAY I LEAVE
THIS WORLD OF WOE,

PASTOR OGLETHORPE. And Miss Maude and Miss Myrtle, you've been so good to me...

THE SANDERS FAMILY.
HALLELJAH, I AM READY NOW TO GO.

PASTOR OGLETHORPE. Like the boys were saying when I was down at the Blue Nose Tavern last night —

(PASTOR OGLETHORPE realizes what he has said. JUNE stops playing and stares at him.
VERA and DENISE stop playing so they can hear what's going on. BURL, STANLEY, and DENNIS keep the song going as best they can.)

BURL, DENNIS & STANLEY.
I'M HAPPY AS I GO ALONG;
I AM READY NOW TO GO;

PASTOR OGLETHORPE. Blue Nose Tavern! Oh, it's not what you think! June! Honey! It's not what you think!

BURL, DENNIS & STANLEY.
JOIN WITH ME AND SING THIS SONG;
I AM READY NOW TO GO.

(JUNE signs, "You went to the Blue Nose Tavern last night?")

PASTOR OGLETHORPE. What?

BURL, DENNIS & STANLEY.
I'M GETTING READY NOW
TO SAIL AWAY

(JUNE signs, "You went to a bar last night?")

PASTOR OGLETHORPE. I don't sign! *(To the congregation.)* What is she saying?

BURL, DENNIS & STANLEY.
TO THE MIGHTY HOME ON HIGH
WHERE I WILL EVER STAY;

(JUNE moves to the back door signing, "Here I am swollen up like a poisoned dog pregnant, and you decide on your last night to go to a bar!")

PASTOR OGLETHORPE. June, honey, I'm sorry —

(JUNE goes out the door. DENISE follows, makes up a sign, and stomps out.)

BURL, DENNIS & STANLEY.
UNTIL THE DAY I LEAVE

(VERA glares at PASTOR OGLETHORPE and follows her two daughters.)

THIS WORLD OF WOE,

PASTOR OGLETHORPE. Wait! *(Turning to the congregation.)* No, Miss Maude, Miss Myrtle, don't leave! It's not what you think! Jasper, Big Head, you were there —

(The SANDERS men flinch at the outing of Jasper and Big Head.)

BURL, DENNIS & STANLEY.
HALLELUJAH, I AM READY NOW TO GO.

PASTOR OGLETHORPE. I can explain! June! Oh, my Mrs. Oglethorpe!

(PASTOR OGLETHORPE rushes off to find his wife. BURL, STANLEY, and DENNIS quickly finish the song.)

BURL, DENNIS & STANLEY.
HALLELUJAH, I AM READY NOW TO GO.
HALLELUJAH, I AM READY NOW TO GO.

DENNIS. We're just gonna take a little break. Stretch our legs. Get some air in here.

(They run out.)

END OF ACT ONE

ACT II

(VERA and DENISE, looking their most pious, ENTER with a sniffly JUNE and usher her to a pew, then stiffly seat themselves. BURL, DENNIS, then STANLEY ENTER and go to their instruments, followed closely by a sheepish PASTOR OGLETHORPE, who goes to the pulpit.)

PASTOR OGLETHORPE. Well, I hope we're all feeling refreshed. *(JUNE stifles a sob.)* And thank you, Sunbeams, for presenting Mrs. Oglethorpe and me with the beautiful going-away gift. I know Mrs. Oglethorpe joins me in saying we will cherish the...

(PASTOR OGLETHORPE doesn't know what it is. Helpless, he looks to JUNE.)

JUNE. *(Weeping)* Bub...Bub...Bub...

(PASTOR OGLETHORPE is lost.)

VERA. *(Steely)* Baby bottle boiler.
PASTOR OGLETHORPE. Baby bottle boiler. I know we'll get a lot of use out of it with this baby and all those to come. *(JUNE cries. To the congregation.)* Oh, and Denise and Donnie wanted me to sincerely apologize for anything of yours that may have been shattered or punctured out there. *(DENISE starts to cry.)* Donnie says if you all will just write your name, address, and the nature of the destruction on a piece of paper, he will gladly and expeditiously make restitution. Donnie thought it best to take Weldon and Eldon on back to the parsonage. *(To DENNIS.)* I'm sorry, Dennis.

49

(To himself.) Who would have thought two little children could cause such ruination? *(JUNE and DENISE dab tears.)* And speaking of ruination, I would like to — *(Leaning toward JUNE.)* — beg for forgiveness for any discomfort my actions might have caused. The Blue Nose Tavern is…uh…not an establishment I was familiar with until last night. Very popular. *(PASTOR OGLETHORPE nods and waves to some men in the congregation.)* Friendly people. Yes, Shelton, Lester, nice to talk to you in the churchyard just now. Wonderful to introduce you to Miss Maude. Miss Myrtle. My mother-in-law. *(VERA sniffs.)* Man is born to trouble —

BURL & DENNIS. Amen.

PASTOR OGLETHORPE. — and who am I to argue? My favorite apostle, Paul, said that every time he tried to do something right it wound up wrong. "For what I will to do, that I do not practice. But what I hate, that I do." That seems to be the fact of my life as well. Christ came into this world to save the sinners, and of them surely I am the worst —

(STANLEY rakes his fingers across the strings of his guitar.)

STANLEY. *(To the congregation.)* You all leave the boy be. He came to the Blue Nose Tavern to get me.

(STANLEY comes forward and sings.)

Song: *COME AROUND*

STANLEY.
IN A LOW AND HUMBLE COTTAGE A MOTHER KNELT TO
    PRAY:
"WATCH OVER LITTLE SONNY, LORD, IF HE SHOULD
    EVER STRAY."
BUT THE WORLD WAS YOUNG AND WILLING, WIDE OPEN
    WAS THE GATE;
HIS MOTHER PRAYED FOR PATIENCE, BUT SONNY COULD
    NOT WAIT.
HIS HEART WAS ALWAYS HOPEFUL, THOUGH HIS AIM
    NOT ALWAYS HIGH;
HIS BODY FULL OF SPIRIT; HIS THROAT WAS SELDOM

DRY.

NOW THERE'S A LITTLE MARKER ON A BAR STOOL 'WAY
    'CROSS TOWN;

IT SAYS "RESERVED FOR SONNY IF HE SHOULD COME
    AROUND"

"COME AROUND, COME AROUND;" OUR SAVIOR HE IS
    PLEADING, "COME AROUND."

"COME TO ME, DON'T DELAY. TAKE UP THE CROSS, MY
    SON, AND NEVER STRAY."

NOW ALL YOU CHRISTIAN PEOPLE, THINK BEFORE YOU
    CAST THAT STONE;

SONNY HAD HIS SHARE OF SIN, BUT SONNY'S NOT
    ALONE.

AND MAYBE THERE'S A MARKER SOMEWHERE ON
    HIGHER GROUND

RESERVED FOR EACH OF US IF WE SHOULD COME
    AROUND.

"COME AROUND, COME AROUND;" OUR SAVIOR HE IS
    PLEADING, "COME AROUND."

"COME TO ME, DON'T DELAY. TAKE UP THE CROSS, MY
    SON, AND NEVER STRAY."

(STANLEY regards the congregation for a beat.)

STANLEY. When Jesus Christ came upon Peter by the Sea of Galilee, He said, "Throw down your nets and follow me." Peter said, "Beats fishing," quit his job, and took off for parts unknown. That's me.

When Jesus walked on the water, the rest were afraid. Peter said, "I can do that," but after the first few steps, his faith flew out from under him and he sank like a stone. That's me. When Christ gathered the disciples and explained that He would be rejected, killed, and rise again, Peter pulled Christ to one side and said, "Buddy, I think I can help you with your story." That's me.

When Jesus warned Peter that Satan was looking to sift him like wheat, Peter said, "No, Lord, I love you so much I would die for you." But three times before the sun rose, Peter swore he'd never met the man. That's me.

Peter was a drifter, a hothead, a know-it-all. He made promises and broke 'em, started things he couldn't finish, made messes he couldn't clean up. But Jesus forgave him, loved him, saved him. *(Motioning to PASTOR OGLETHORPE.)* That's him. Your Reverend Oglethorpe sat with me last night at the Blue Nose Tavern. And where everyone else sees nothing but a lost cause, Mervin took the chance to spread a little grace.

Last time I was here, I had left the family and gone out singing on my own 'cause I was better than them and they were holding me back. Last time I was here, I was in the movies, but I quit 'cause I got better things to do than stand around and wait for Gene Autry. Last time I was here, I was making records, but some man in a tie wanted to tell me what to sing, and nobody tells me what to do. Last time I was here, I was on the bill with the big-name groups, but management and I didn't see eye-to-eye and they got tired of bailing me out. 'Cause, you know, there's a Blue Nose Tavern in every little town.

Now I play where they'll have me and I sing what they want. Traveling songs, courtin' songs, I-done-wrong songs, and I-been-done-wrong songs. But they don't want to hear gospel songs. 'Cause gospel songs make them remember, and the men hang their heads and the women cry.

Sometimes it's not a big thing that knocks you down. How many times have I started over? How many chances have I lost? Always saying tomorrow. Tomorrow I'll do better. But I don't. *(Laughing)* Have you heard the one about the preacher who walked into a bar? Mervin about cleared the place out last night. You've never seen so much ducking and tip-toeing. Some flat-out scorched a path to the door. *(To PASTOR OGLETHORPE.)* I bet Luther's sorry he called you, you hurt his business so bad. *(To congregation.)* I'd have run, too, but the boy's bald-faced grit caught me by the coattails. Old Mervin here pulled up a chair, ordered up an Orange Crush, shelled a few peanuts, and told me stories about that rascal Peter.

Ever since the war ended, something's been pulling me back here hard. This last month I've been all through these parts, dodging and weaseling around trying to make it all the way home. I tangled with it all day today and determined to head back for parts west.

But I came here. If Peter messed up that bad and our Savior

still asked him to look after his sheep, maybe there's a prayer for me. *(To PASTOR OGLETHORPE.)* What I most appreciate is that you got me to these back steps tonight.

I about believe the only thing that will save me is the Gospel. Singing these songs like we did when life didn't look so beaten up and blue.

When Peter finally turned back toward Christ, Jesus charged him to help his brother. *(To BURL.)* Brother, I don't know how much help I can be to you, but you sure could save this ol' boy right now. You talked about the Sanders Family starting out as three. Looks like you're gonna be short a few hands. It would be a blessing to me if we could go back to that number.

(STANLEY starts to sing, then is joined by the family.)

Song: *I'LL LIVE AGAIN*

STANLEY.
IF, SOME MORNING, I AM GONE
FROM THIS VALE OF TEARS,
I'M GOING HOME TO LIVE AGAIN;

STANLEY AND BURL.
I AM GOING ON A TRIP
WHEN I SAY GOODBYE;
I'LL LIVE AGAIN

THE SANDERS FAMILY.
OVER ON THE OTHER SIDE.

(During the song, PASTOR OGLETHORPE scurries to help JUNE get her instruments. She, in turn, allows him to play the tambourine with her. They're both relieved that their tiff is over.)

THE SANDERS FAMILY & PASTOR OGLETHORPE.
I'LL LIVE AGAIN OVER ON THE GOLDEN STRAND;
I'LL SING AND SHOUT WITH THE MIGHTY ANGEL BAND;
YOU'LL SEE ME RISE BEYOND THE STARRY SKIES;
I'LL LIVE AGAIN OVER ON THE OTHER SIDE.

VERA.
I'VE A MANSION OVER THERE, BUILT IN BEAUTY RARE;

VERA & STANLEY.
I'M GOING HOME TO LIVE AGAIN;

VERA, STANLEY & BURL.
WHEN THEY LAY ME IN THE GRAVE, DON'T YOU WEEP
    FOR ME;
I'LL LIVE AGAIN
THE SANDERS FAMILY.
OVER ON THE OTHER SIDE.

THE SANDERS FAMILY & PASTOR OGLETHORPE.
I'LL LIVE AGAIN OVER ON THE GOLDEN STRAND;
I'LL SING AND SHOUT WITH THE MIGHTY ANGEL BAND;
YOU'LL SEE ME RISE BEYOND THE STARRY SKIES;
I'LL LIVE AGAIN OVER ON THE OTHER SIDE.
I'LL LIVE AGAIN OVER ON THE GOLDEN STRAND;
I'LL SING AND SHOUT WITH THE MIGHTY ANGEL BAND;
YOU'LL SEE ME RISE BEYOND THE STARRY SKIES;
I'LL LIVE AGAIN OVER ON THE OTHER SIDE.
I'LL LIVE AGAIN OVER ON THE OTHER SIDE.

*(After the song, PASTOR OGLETHORPE excitedly gestures to the
    family.)*

PASTOR OGLETHORPE. Make a circle, make a circle.

*(The family, bewildered, sits in a circle in front of the pulpit as PAS-
    TOR OGLETHORPE rushes into his office.)*

BURL. *(To JUNE.)* Do you know what this is?
JUNE. I have no idea.
STANLEY. Well, he's always got something.

*(PASTOR OGLETHORPE opens the door and strikes a pose. He is
    wearing a ten-gallon hat and his accordion. He joins the fam-
    ily in the middle of the circle.)*

Song: *ROUND-UP IN THE SKY*

PASTOR OGLETHORPE.

I AM AN ORPHAN DOGIE; I CAME UP PRETTY ROUGH
SCROUNGING ON THE PRAIRIE, I NEVER HAD ENOUGH;
I FELL IN WITH THE DEVIL, FLEECIN' STEERS AND
    GOATS;
HE TIED A BELL AROUND MY NECK AND FATTENED ME
    WITH OATS.
NOW SATAN IS A CHARMER, BUT THIS I COULD NOT SEE
UNTIL THE DAY I FOUND OUT THAT HE WAS FLEECIN' ME;
HE STRUNG ME UP ABOVE THE BLOCK; I'D GIVEN UP ALL
    HOPE;
HIS BUTCHER KNIFE WAS READY, BUT JESUS CUT THE
    ROPE.
HALLELUJAH, TI-YIPPIE-YIPPIE-YO-YIPPIE-YAY,
HALLELUJAH, TI-YIPPIE-YIPPIE-YI
WHEN THE HERDS NO LONGER ROAM
AND THE DOGIES FIND A HOME
AT THE ROUND-UP IN THE SKY.
YES, JESUS IS A COWBOY; HE RIDES THE LONE PRAIRIE
ROPING STRAYS AND STRAGGLERS; THAT'S HOW HE
    FOUND ME;
HE LASSOED ME THAT EVENING; HE PINNED ME IN THE
    DUST;
HE BRANDED ME WITH A DOUBLE B: "BEULAHLAND OR
    BUST"

THE SANDERS FAMILY & PASTOR OGLETHORPE.

HALLELUJAH, TI-YIPPIE-YIPPIE-YO-YIPPIE-YAY,
HALLELUJAH, TI-YIPPIE-YIPPIE-YI
WHEN THE HERDS NO LONGER ROAM
AND THE DOGIES FIND A HOME
AT THE ROUND-UP IN THE SKY.

PASTOR OGLETHORPE.

COME ALL YOU ORPHAN DOGIES WITHOUT NO EARTHLY
    DAD;

YOU'VE GOT A HEAV'NLY FATHER, SO DON'T FEEL LOST
    AND SAD;
THERE IS A RANCH IN GLORY; IT'S HAPPY AND IT'S FULL
WITH JESUS AS THE FOREMAN, AND HE DON'T TAKE NO
    BULL.

THE SANDERS FAMILY & PASTOR OGLETHORPE.
HALLELUJAH, TI-YIPPIE-YIPPIE-YO-YIPPIE-YAY,
HALLELUJAH, TI-YIPPIE-YIPPIE-YI
WHEN THE HERDS NO LONGER ROAM
AND THE DOGIES FIND A HOME
AT THE ROUND-UP IN THE SKY.

PASTOR OGLETHORPE.
OH-LAY-HO-DE-LAY-HEE
OH-LAY-HO-DE-LAY-HEE
YO-DE-LAY-HEE-HOO
YO-DE-LAY-HEE-HOO
YO-DE-LAY-HEE-HOO
YO-DE-LAY-HEE-HOO
YO-DE-LAY-HEE-HOO
YO-DE-LAY-HEE-HOO
YO-DE-LAY-HEE-HOO
AND YOUR DOGIES, TOO
YO-DE-LAY-HE-HO-HE-LAY-HE-HO-HE-HOO-OO.

*(Exhausted from all the yodeling, PASTOR OGLETHORPE sinks
down beside JUNE. They hold hands and she puts her head on
his shoulder during the next song.)*

Song: *I LOVE TO TELL THE STORY*

THE SANDERS FAMILY.
I LOVE TO TELL THE STORY
OF UNSEEN THINGS ABOVE,
OF JESUS AND HIS GLORY,
OF JESUS AND HIS LOVE;
I LOVE TO TELL THE STORY
BECAUSE I KNOW 'TIS TRUE;

IT SATISFIES MY LONGINGS
AS NOTHING ELSE CAN DO.
I LOVE TO TELL THE STORY;
'TWILL BE MY THEME IN GLORY,
TO TELL THE OLD, OLD STORY
OF JESUS AND HIS LOVE.

VERA.
I LOVE TO TELL THE STORY;
MORE WONDERFUL IT SEEMS
THAN ALL THE GOLDEN FANCIES
OF ALL OUR GOLDEN DREAMS.
AND WHEN IN SCENES OF GLORY
I SING THE NEW, NEW SONG,
'TWILL BE THE OLD, OLD STORY
THAT I HAVE LOVED SO LONG.

THE SANDERS FAMILY.
I LOVE TO TELL THE STORY;
'TWILL BE MY THEME IN GLORY,
TO TELL THE OLD, OLD STORY
OF JESUS AND HIS LOVE.

(VERA gathers a bag and comes forward.)

VERA. And Jesus said, "Suffer the little children to come unto me." Amen. What a blessing to see so many of God's precious angels scattered among the congregation tonight. You know, I'm not only the mother of three, but soon to be the grandmother of three. And if Dennis would get on the stick, I'd have hope for more. But I don't have to tell all you mothers out there our greatest gift is patience. So, of course, it fell on me to do the children's devotional tonight. So, quick, children, scoot up to the edge of your pews. This is for you.

The other day, I was minding my own business peeling potatoes when a great big airplane fell out of the sky and landed in my sweet corn patch! I'm standing at the sink and there goes an airplane whizzing by my kitchen window so low, I can see the little man in there flying the thing. And I said, "Lord have mercy, he's gonna crash!" I run out the door and start hollering for Burl.

BURL. I was in the toolshed when I heard his engine sputter out.

VERA. We take off running after it, and it hit the ground and started tearing through corn — wings and stalks and cobs flying. Burl and I are jumping and tripping, hoping we can save him, get to him before the thing blows him and us to bits. Pull his shattered body out of the wreckage. But when we get up to the cockpit, we hear a rattling and a cussing so blue it about melted the buttons off my housedress. And out pops this little man's head, and he says he's so sorry. He ran out of gas. Ran out of gas, children. Think on this. What kind of nuthead flings himself into the air and forgets to put gasoline in the plane? Well, I can guarantee there's no way he's right with Jesus. His language was nothing but shameful, and that's something I never want you to do. Dirty talk and taking the Lord's name in vain is a sin. And sin sends you to where? Everlasting Hell. Pitch black and teeth-grinding pain.

But while I was shucking the few ears that weren't mashed flat, God put me to thinking on this airplane. And God in His wondrous way let me see that we, too, are airplanes in this world. And life is God's big airshow! And we have a choice. Use Jesus as your gasoline and delight the crowd with loop-de-loops or take your chances and crash and burn in the vegetables.

And the Lord's message was so clear, I had Burl run down to the dime store and get us some toy planes for our witness tonight.

BURL. I enjoyed it.

(VERA pulls a paper airplane out of the bag.)

VERA. Now, this one I made. What do you call this? A paper airplane. Fold, fold, fold just so. The paper airplane is like the soul we are born with. Plain paper, simple, good intentions. Let's see how it flies. *(VERA launches the paper airplane toward the congregation.)* Oh dear, that was a short trip, wasn't it? Kind of went every whichaway, and as soon as it got in the air, it crashed. That's life without the Lord. How are we going to fix this? Anybody? Get a better plane! *(VERA pulls out a balsa wood glider.)* Oh, look at this! A glider! Light as a feather, fancy wings - and what does this say? — Aerodynamic! That sounds good! Let's see how this plane flies.

(VERA lofts the glider into the air.) Oh well, that was a little better. It kind of went the way I wanted, but it still crashed. Now, what do my paper airplane and my glider have in common? My arm! They can only fly if I throw them in the air. And what is my arm, children? Self-will! But what if we take my arm out of it and let Jesus supply the power? How high and straight could we go? *(VERA pulls out a rubber-band plane.)* Oh, look at this! This plane has a propeller and a rubber band engine. Just like Jesus! Look, Jesus is so confident, he's put little wheels to land on. Let's see how this plane flies. *(VERA begins to wind up the plane.)* We just wind it up like this. So simple. And look at it go! *(The plane crashes to the floor. VERA picks it up and winds it with a vengeance.)* With the Lord as our power, we can go anywhere! High above the clouds, looking down on the heathens and sinners. They're just specks. The devil's arm isn't long enough — *(Pop! The rubber band snaps VERA's hand so hard she has to turn her back to the congregation to keep from yelping. She hops from one foot to the other to manage the pain. After she gathers herself, with her back still to the congregation, she begins winding the toy again.)* With the Lord as our power, we'll be up there skimming heaven, winking at the angels. *(Accusingly, to BURL.)* Have you been playing with this? *(BURL shakes his head no. VERA continues to wind.)* Maybe it's one of those smoke-writing planes. Yes! A smoke-writing plane — *(Turning back toward the congregation, winding the plane.)* — and we can write in puffy letters — *(Pop! The band snaps VERA, and without thinking, she violently throws the plane to the floor and stomps it. A long beat.)* Let us pray. Heavenly Father, thank you for giving us gas and always keeping our tanks full. *(The family, stifling laughter, sings "Jesus, Savior, Pilot Me" under VERA's prayer.)* Lead us not into the cornfields of life, but help us to fly straight into your arms where there is no pain whatsoever. May the rubber bands of sin become limp within us, and may our wings be so aerodynamic that we brush the clouds for all eternity. We ask this in Thy name. Amen.

(The family starts the Prophet Medley as PASTOR OGLETHORPE picks up the shattered pieces of the airplane.)

Song: *DANIEL IN THE LION'S DEN*

DENNIS & DENISE.
WHEN I WAS YOUNG, I WENT TO SUNDAY SCHOOL;
I LEARNED THE TEN COMMANDMENTS AND THE
   GOLDEN RULE;

THE SANDERS FAMILY.
I HEARD HOW PROPHETS OF OLD LEARNED TO WALK IN
   GOD'S WAY;
GOD WAS THERE IN DAYS OF OLD, AND HE'S HERE
   TODAY.

BURL & STANLEY.
HE WAS THERE WITH

THE SANDERS FAMILY.
DANIEL IN THE LION'S DEN;

BURL & STANLEY.
HE WAS

THE SANDERS FAMILY.
IN THE WHALE WITH JONAH;

BURL & STANLEY.
MOSES

THE SANDERS FAMILY.
AND THE BURNING BUSH;
FORTY DAYS AND NIGHTS

BURL & STANLEY.
WITH NOAH;

THE SANDERS FAMILY.
JOSEPH READ PHARAOH'S DREAMS
'CAUSE GOD HELPED HIM SEE;

BURL & STANLEY.
HE WAS THERE WITH

THE SANDERS FAMILY.
DANIEL IN THE LION'S DEN,
AND HE'S HERE WITH ME.

Song: *EZEKIEL SAW THE WHEEL*

THE SANDERS FAMILY.
WELL, EZEKIEL SAW THE WHEEL

STANLEY.
A-TURNIN'

THE SANDERS FAMILY.
WAY UP IN THE MIDDLE OF THE AIR;
EZEKIEL SAW THE WHEEL

STANLEY.
A-TURNIN'

THE SANDERS FAMILY.
WAY IN THE MIDDLE OF THE AIR.
WELL, THE LITTLE WHEEL RUNS BY FAITH,
AND THE BIG WHEEL RUNS BY THE GRACE OF GOD;
IT'S A WHEEL, IT'S A WHEEL WAY IN THE MIDDLE OF THE
    AIR.

BURL.
EZEKIEL SAW THE WHEEL OF TIME

THE SANDERS FAMILY.
WAY IN THE MIDDLE OF THE AIR;

BURL.
EVERY SPOKE WAS A HUMANKIND

THE SANDERS FAMILY.
WAY IN THE MIDDLE OF THE AIR.
WELL, EZEKIEL SAW THE WHEEL

STANLEY.
A-TURNIN'

THE SANDERS FAMILY.
WAY UP IN THE MIDDLE OF THE AIR;
EZEKIEL SAW THE WHEEL

STANLEY.
A-TURNIN'

THE SANDERS FAMILY.
WAY IN THE MIDDLE OF THE AIR.
WELL, THE LITTLE WHEEL RUNS BY FAITH,
AND THE BIG WHEEL RUNS BY THE GRACE OF GOD;
IT'S A WHEEL, IT'S A WHEEL WAY IN THE MIDDLE OF THE
    AIR.

Song: *WE ARE CLIMBING JACOB'S LADDER*

VERA, DENNIS & DENISE.
WE ARE CLIMBING JACOB'S LADDER,
WE ARE CLIMBING JACOB'S LADDER,
WE ARE CLIMBING JACOB'S LADDER,
SOLDIERS OF THE CROSS.
LOVE WILL LIFT US HIGHER AND HIGHER,
LOVE WILL LIFT US HIGHER AND HIGHER,
LOVE WILL LIFT US HIGHER, HIGHER,
BROTHERS, SISTERS, ALL,
BROTHERS, SISTERS, ALL.

Song: *JOSHUA FIT THE BATTLE OF JERICHO*

DENNIS.
JOSHUA FIT THE BATTLE OF

THE SANDERS FAMILY.
JERICHO, JERICHO, JERICHO;

DENNIS.
JOSHUA FIT THE BATTLE OF

THE SANDERS FAMILY.
JERICHO,
AND THE WALLS CAME A-TUMBLING DOWN.

DENNIS.
NOW THE LORD COMMANDED JOSHUA,
"I COMMAND YOU AND OBEY YOU MUST;
YOU JUST MARCH STRAIGHT UP TO THOSE CITY WALLS
AND THE WALLS WILL TURN TO DUST."

BURL & STANLEY.
THAT MORNING WHEN

DENNIS.
JOSHUA FIT THE BATTLE OF

THE SANDERS FAMILY.
JERICHO, JERICHO, JERICHO;

DENNIS.
JOSHUA FIT THE BATTLE OF

THE SANDERS FAMILY.
JERICHO,
AND THE WALLS CAME A-TUMBLING DOWN.

DENNIS.
STRAIGHT UP TO THE WALLS OF JERICHO,
HE MARCHED WITH A SPEAR IN HAND,
"GO BLOW THAT RAM'S HORN," JOSHUA CRIED,
"FOR THE BATTLE IS IN MY HAND."

BURL & STANLEY.
THAT MORNING WHEN

DENNIS.
JOSHUA FIT THE BATTLE OF

THE SANDERS FAMILY.
JERICHO, JERICHO, JERICHO;

DENNIS.
JOSHUA FIT THE BATTLE OF

THE SANDERS FAMILY.
JERICHO,
AND THE WALLS CAME A-TUMBLING DOWN.

DENNIS.
THE LAMB-RAM-SHEEP HORNS BEGAN TO BLOW,
AND THE TRUMPETS BEGAN TO SOUND,

(JUNE blows a horn.)

AND JOSHUA COMMANDED, "NOW CHILDREN, SHOUT!"
AND THE WALLS CAME TUMBLING DOWN.

BURL & STANLEY.
THAT MORNING WHEN

DENNIS.
JOSHUA FIT THE BATTLE OF

THE SANDERS FAMILY.
JERICHO, JERICHO, JERICHO;

DENNIS.
JOSHUA FIT THE BATTLE OF

THE SANDERS FAMILY.
JERICHO,

AND THE WALLS CAME A-TUMBLING DOWN.
AND THE WALLS CAME A-TUMBLING DOWN.
THE WALLS CAME TUMBLING DOWN.

DENNIS. June...

(PASTOR OGLETHORPE runs over to help JUNE up.)

JUNE. I'm fine.
PASTOR OGLETHORPE. My Mrs. Oglethorpe.
JUNE. I've been sitting here listening to the goodbye songs and the goodbye wishes, and I've been trying so hard to memorize the faces of you dear, good people.

Tomorrow morning, I will unmake the bed. The bed I have called mine since I've been called Mrs. Oglethorpe. And my heaped-up heart swings from jelly-like and scared to pins-and-needles rarin'-to-go. I'm what's called expecting. And I've never expected so much in my whole life.

When Denise and I were little, we'd play the Sears and Roebuck game. Let the catalog fall open where it may. You get what's on your page, I get what's on mine. And the adventures we had! Oh, the parties we attended in our white gloves and smart outfits. They served punch! And our homes were decorated. We had curtains with string pulls and pictures of Paris and little pillows you put on the davenport just for show. Denise's home was in Raleigh or Charleston or Atlanta. I always built mine right beside Mama and Daddy.

Mama and Daddy let us children grow up like bantams. We despised shoes, lived in the woods, we dug tunnels and built forts and dared each other to swing from scuppernong vines. But we always knew there was home. Sitting on Grandma's lap while she tasted our tears, leaning against Daddy's arm while he's reading the newspaper, Mama scraping an apple with a spoon when my throat was sore. Knowing full well that God has a-hold of their hearts and their lives bear His eternal fingerprints. I can go anywhere, 'cause their fingerprints are all over me.

God dreams much bigger dreams for us than we ever dream for ourselves. Don't be mad, Mama. Mervin's not dragging me off from home. I believe God has called us to Wildorado. I believe God will be sitting in the pew with me listening to Mervin bring the Gospel to those lonesome cowboys. I believe God will teach me how to make chile con carne and chicken-fried steak. I believe God means for me to sign for the deaf, and someday someone out there is going to understand me. And when I pull the covers up around my neck in Texas, I believe God will be there and He will say this is good. Where God is, there is home. *(To DENNIS.)*...I'm done.

(DENNIS rises.)

    DENNIS. "And Paul took leave of his brethren...
    DENNIS & JUNE. "He bade them farewell, saying,
    THE SANDERS FAMILY & PASTOR OGLETHORPE. *(Standing)* "I will return again unto you, if God will. Now be of good cheer, for there stands by me this night the angel of God, whose I am, and whom I serve."

        Song: *JUST OVER IN THE GLORYLAND*

    THE SANDERS FAMILY & PASTOR OGLETHORPE.
I'VE A HOME PREPARED WHERE THE SAINTS ABIDE,
JUST OVER IN THE GLORYLAND;
AND I LONG TO BE BY MY SAVIOR'S SIDE,
JUST OVER IN THE GLORYLAND.
JUST OVER IN THE GLORYLAND,
I'LL JOIN THE HAPPY ANGEL BAND
JUST OVER IN THE GLORYLAND;
JUST OVER IN THE GLORYLAND,
THERE WITH THE MIGHTY HOST I'LL STAND,
JUST OVER IN THE GLORYLAND.

    BURL & VERA.
I AM ON MY WAY TO THOSE MANSIONS FAIR,
JUST OVER IN THE GLORYLAND;

    DENNIS & DENISE.
THERE TO SING GOD'S PRAISE AND HIS GLORY SHARE,
JUST OVER IN THE GLORYLAND.

THE SANDERS FAMILY & PASTOR OGLETHORPE.
JUST OVER IN THE GLORYLAND,
I'LL JOIN THE HAPPY ANGEL BAND
JUST OVER IN THE GLORYLAND;
JUST OVER IN THE GLORYLAND,
THERE WITH THE MIGHTY HOST I'LL STAND,
JUST OVER IN THE GLORYLAND.
JUST OVER IN THE GLORYLAND,
I'LL JOIN THE HAPPY ANGEL BAND
JUST OVER IN THE GLORYLAND;
JUST OVER IN THE GLORYLAND,
THERE WITH THE MIGHTY HOST I'LL STAND,
JUST OVER IN THE GLORYLAND.
JUST OVER IN THE GLORYLAND,
I'LL JOIN THE HAPPY ANGEL BAND
JUST OVER IN THE GLORYLAND;
JUST OVER IN THE GLORYLAND,
THERE WITH THE MIGHTY HOST I'LL STAND,
JUST OVER IN THE GLORYLAND.
JUST OVER IN THE GLORYLAND.

BURL. Thank you, Mount Pleasant. Thank you all for having us. And Mervin, we wish you and June a safe trip, and God bless your new church.
PASTOR OGLETHORPE. Thank you, Burl. Thank you, family. Thank you, Mount Pleasant. *(Shaking DENNIS's hand.)* And Reverend Sanders, welcome home, *(PASTOR OGLETHORPE puts his hat on.)* Wildorado, here we come! I've got spurs on my boots and burrs under my saddle!

Song: *UNCLOUDED DAY*

THE SANDERS FAMILY & PASTOR OGLETHORPE.
OH, THEY TELL ME OF A HOME FAR BEYOND THE SKIES,
OH, THEY TELL ME OF A HOME FAR AWAY;
OH, THEY TELL ME OF A HOME WHERE NO STORM
    CLOUDS RISE,
OH, THEY TELL ME OF AN UNCLOUDED DAY.
OH, THE LAND OF CLOUDLESS DAY,

OH, THE LAND OF AN UNCLOUDED SKY;
OH, THEY TELL ME OF A HOME WHERE NO STORM
    CLOUDS RISE,
OH, THEY TELL ME OF AN UNCLOUDED DAY.
OH, THE LAND OF CLOUDLESS DAY,
OH, THE LAND OF AN UNCLOUDED SKY;
OH, THEY TELL ME OF A HOME WHERE NO STORM
    CLOUDS RISE,
OH, THEY TELL ME OF AN UNCLOUDED DAY.

*(The family EXITS through the congregation. PASTOR OGLETHORPE
    calls them back for one more.)*

Song: *DO LORD*

THE SANDERS FAMILY & PASTOR OGLETHORPE.
DO LORD, OH DO LORD, OH DO REMEMBER ME,
DO LORD, OH DO LORD, OH DO REMEMBER ME,
DO LORD, OH DO LORD, OH DO REMEMBER ME,
LOOK AWAY BEYOND THE BLUE.
I'VE GOT A HOME IN GLORYLAND THAT OUTSHINES THE
    SUN,
I'VE GOT A HOME IN GLORYLAND THAT OUTSHINES THE
    SUN,
I'VE GOT A HOME IN GLORYLAND THAT OUTSHINES THE
    SUN,
LOOK AWAY BEYOND THE BLUE.

*(JUNE stops playing and stands perfectly still. She stares straight
    ahead for several beats, then moves to PASTOR OGLETHORPE
    and tries to get his attention. It's not easy.)*

Song: *DO LORD*

THE SANDERS FAMILY & PASTOR OGLETHORPE.
DO LORD, OH DO LORD, OH DO REMEMBER ME,
DO LORD, OH DO LORD, OH DO REMEMBER ME,
DO LORD, OH DO LORD, OH DO REMEMBER ME,
LOOK AWAY BEYOND THE BLUE.

(Finally, JUNE whispers into PASTOR OGLETHORPE'S ear. He is too shocked to move. JUNE whispers again. PASTOR OGLETHORPE hugs her. She gestures that they should go.)

THE SANDERS FAMILY.
I TOOK JESUS AS MY SAVIOR, YOU TAKE HIM TOO,

(PASTOR OGLETHORPE crosses and whispers to BURL.)

I TOOK JESUS AS MY SAVIOR, YOU TAKE HIM TOO,

(BURL whispers to VERA. Everyone gets excited. The family speeds up the song, racing to the ending.)

I TOOK JESUS AS MY SAVIOR, YOU TAKE HIM TOO,
LOOK AWAY BEYOND THE BLUE.
DO LORD, OH DO LORD, OH DO REMEMBER ME,
DO LORD, OH DO LORD, OH DO REMEMBER ME,
DO LORD, OH DO LORD, OH DO REMEMBER ME,
LOOK AWAY BEYOND THE BLUE.

(PASTOR OGLETHORPE and the family gather JUNE and walk her out the onstage door.
After a few moments, PASTOR OGLETHORPE bursts back through the door and grabs the pink suitcase, pressing it to his chest.)

PASTOR OGLETHORPE. *(To the congregation.)* I'm going to be a daddy!

(He runs out.)

THE END

PROPERTY PLOT

FURNITURE
1 SR pew
2 SL pews
1 UC pew
Piano stool (swivel)
Stove
Offering table
Pulpit
Hymnal rack
Cymbal stand for 1 cymbal

HAND PROPS
1 practical hymnal — fits in Vera's purse
Mervin's hand Bible
Dennis's hand Bible
Mervin's note cards (3 x 5 white)
Mervin's pocket comb (black)
Pink overnight bag
Toy piano
Dinner bell
2 sparkly bowties
Ball to make offstage noise
Crash box to make offstage noise
1 twin's outfit
Vera's purse
Paper bag with airplanes
Four-folded paper airplane made of notebook paper
Balsa-wood glider
Balsa-wood airplane with rubber band-powered propeller and landing wheels
2 glasses of water (hidden onstage for cast)
Handkerchiefs

STAGE DRESSING
2 wall sconces
Church attendance sign

Office wall calendar
Office wall painting
3 hymnals (secured in hymnal rack)
Hanging light bulb
Wall light switch for hanging light bulb

INSTRUMENTS
TO INCLUDE ANY OF THE FOLLOWING:
Piano
Guitars
Banjo
Mandolin
Stand-up bass
Fiddle
Autoharp
Ukulele
Accordion
Horn (trumpet, cornet, or bugle)

PERCUSSION INSTRUMENTS
Wooden spoons
Tambourine
Washboard with scrub brush
Cymbal
Basket (wicker with beans)
Triangle
Drumsticks and mallets

NOTE: In order to ensure that the propeller plane does not fly, the original rubber band should be replaced with one that is slightly longer. A longer rubber band guarantees that the actress can wind the plane up as long as she wants without actually popping the band. All rubber band-popping is acted, not actual pain.

COSTUME PLOT

VERA SANDERS
    Pattern dress
    Sweater
    Cotton lisle stockings
    Garter belt
    Lace-up shoes
    Hat with hatpin
    Handbag
    Wedding ring
    Handkerchief

JUNE SANDERS
    Maternity dress
    Maternity pad
    Light overcoat
    Off-white socks
    Lace-up shoes
    Round-lens eyeglasses

DENISE SANDERS
    Shirtwaist dress
    Stockings
    Garter belt
    Pumps

MERVIN OGLETHORPE
    2-piece blue pinstripe suit
    Brown vest
    White shirt
    String tie
    Western boots
    White handkerchief
    Ten-gallon hat

BURL SANDERS
- White collarless shirt
- Gold collar button
- Plaid vest
- Striped pants
- Striped suspenders
- Lace-up shoes
- Tweed suit jacket
- Hat

STANLEY SANDERS
- Shirt
- Suit jacket
- Pants
- Suspenders
- Cap
- Ankle boots

DENNIS SANDERS
- Suit
- White shirt
- Pattern tie
- Lace-up shoes

Howard Crabtree's
When Pigs Fly

Conceived by
HOWARD CRABTREE
and
MARK WALDROP

Sketches and Lyrics by
MARK WALDROP

Music by
DICK GALLAGHER

"Exceptionally cheerful, militantly gay musical
review [with] hilarity, wit and outre humor."
The New York Times

"Campy revue soars to silly heights.... Waldrop's
lyrics are skillful and funny."
New York Daily News

"Could have your eyes out on stalks....
The music is glitter bright and tuneful."
New York Post

In this side-splitting musical extravaganza by the creators of
Howard Crabtree's Whoop-Dee-Doo!, new heights of hilar-
ity are achieved in each outrageous skit. During its long Off
Broadway run, it won two Drama Desk awards, including
Best Musical Revue, and two Outer Critics Circle awards,
including Best Off-Broadway musical. 5 m. (#25239)

MUSICALS WITH CHRISTMAS SPIRIT

SCROOGE!

BOOK, MUSIC AND LYRICS BY
Leslie Bricusse

"Wonderful theatre."
Yorkshire Evening Post

"Sensational.... It was terrific."
BBC Radio

"Just wait until you see *Scrooge!*"
Radio 3 – Australia

This is the wildly successful stage version of the classical movie musical based on *A Christmas Carol* which starred Albert Finney. Adapted by a renowned writer-composer-lyricist, it is an easy-to-produce show to delight audiences during the holiday season. CD available. (#21029)

Sanders Family Christmas

WRITTEN BY	CONCEIVED BY
Connie Ray	**Alan Bailey**

MUSICAL ARRANGEMENTS BY
John Foley & Gary Fagin

From the creators of the
"perfectly delightful,"[1] "totally beguiling,"[2]
"charming and funny"[3] musical comedy
SMOKE ON THE MOUNTAIN

It's December 24, 1941, and America is going to war. So is Dennis Sanders of the Sanders Family Singers. Join Pastor Mervin Oglethorpe and the memorable Sanders family as they evoke some down-home Christmas cheer with hilarious, touching stories and 25 bluegrass Christmas songs. Here is a richly entertaining musical that has audiences clapping, stomping and singing along with the *SMOKE ON THE MOUNTAIN* crowd. (#20948)

[1 *The New Yorker*, 2 *The New York Times*, 3 *New York Post*]